ENDORSEMENTS

How often can you say I'm better for having read a book? I can! Steve Sanders' *Love: The Greatest of These* is that book. Tackling a central theme of Scripture, Sanders explores the biblical message of "love" in a most practical manner. Without watering down the spiritual power, significance or personal challenge of the concept, *Love: The Greatest of These* introduces eternal truths via a well-crafted, relevant and impactful story. There's never a bad time to embrace love. This book is a great place to start.

Phillip Van Hooser

Keynote Speaker, Trainer and Leadership Authority
Author of We Need To Talk: Building Trust When
Communicating Gets Critical

I have known Steve Sanders for many years as a friend. One thing I have known about Steve is his love for the Word of God and his depth of scholarship in his studies. But I never knew of his skill as a storyteller. The reader of this book is in for a double treat: A story that will capture your heart AND the best introduction to the Biblical teaching on the Fruit of the Spirit (specifically the Fruit of Love) that I have ever seen. Reading it, I found myself identifying with the main character. I also found myself being convicted (not condemned) by the truth I was reading. Get ready for a good story – and an encounter with God's truth.

David Parish

President, World Missions and Evangelism, Inc.

In *Love, The Greatest of These*, Steve Sanders will take you on a captivating journey of spiritual transformation through the power of story. With relatable characters, authentic struggles, and profound biblical insights, Steve's book is a must-read for anyone seeking to deepen their understanding and practice of Christ-like love.

Bob Tiede
CEO, LeadingWithQuestions.com

As someone who has dedicated my career to helping people turn setbacks into comebacks, I was deeply moved by how Steve Sanders has so aptly written a book that demonstrates the resilience and redemptive potential of the human spirit. And, how a person can have exponential growth, especially when they are rooted in God's unfailing love. Sanders' book is a powerful testament to the fact that no matter how far you fall and how hard you land, you can stage a stellar comeback! Plus, no matter how much you have struggled, God's love has the power to transform that struggle into strength and success! This book will inspire you, uplift you and empower you! Read it and share it; you will be blessed and will also be a blessing to others!

Dr. Willie Jolley
*Hall of Fame Speaker, Sirius XM Host, Best Selling Author of
A Setback Is A Setup For A Comeback, and An Attitude of
Excellence*

THE Greatest OF These

by

STEVE SANDERS

LEADERSHIP
Thoughtful, Relevant Leaders From Around The World
BOOKS

DEDICATION

To my friends and first mentors of my adult life, Barry and Shirley Sharp. God placed you in my life at a pivotal point, and your lives and ministry to me are integral to the person I've become today. You set an example for me and Charity and showed us the life of Christian love in a way we could follow.

Barry, I still remember the time I called you late at night – too late. Finding myself at the end of all hope, I asked if I could come by to talk. For a long while, we sat together at your table as you patiently listened to my troubles. I'll never forget your question to me, "Do you want me to tell you what you want to hear or what you need to hear?" Thank you for telling me what I "needed to hear." I doubt that you realize your true impact, and I truly believe God orchestrated it all. Thank you, my friends. May God bless you in all you do!

ACKNOWLEDGEMENTS

Let me begin by just saying "Thank you." I can't possibly name every person who has played a role in my Christian journey, and at times I didn't realize the role you played until years later.

To my wife, Charity, thank you for supporting me in all my endeavors, especially in writing *The Mentor's Map Series!* Your Christlike example to me has been crucial in making God and our church family an essential part of my life.

To my children and grandchildren, I love you more than words can say, and God has blessed me with you. I hope to live my life as an example to you, but more than that, I pray your relationship with the Lord grows day by day. Make Jesus your priority. Nothing is more important.

To my parents and all my family, thank you for prioritizing God and faith during my formative years of life.

To Essie, Candace, Jayce, and Jeanne, I'll never forget our mission trips together. Jeanne, I appreciate your many years of dedication to our home-based church. We've seen our faith mature together as we regularly explore the depths of the scriptures.

To Dr. Michael Heiser, you changed the way I read the Bible forever. I only wish I had been able to learn more from you before you were called home.

To all my pastors along the way and especially Brothers J.T. and David Parish. At just the right time, both of you were there for me and I grew immensely under your teaching. Brother J.T., I know you're rejoicing in God's presence today.

And finally, to all the Noble Bereans out there – reflect God well!

TABLE OF CONTENTS

Prologue...xiii

A Jaded View 1

Reconsidering Life 7

A Memorable Coffee 11

The First Test 17

The First Big Stumble...23

August Refocused 29

It's My Party...37

Unrealized Expectations 43

Rethinking Honor...47

Baby Steps 51

More to the Story 55

The Interruption...61

Seeing the Best in Others 65

Losing It 71

Lost It...77

The Worst Celebration 81

A Different Way...85

Crossed the Line 89

Real Change..93

Passing the Torch...95

Meet the Author...99

PREFACE

Back in 2013, I led a small, home-based church group which embarked on a mission trip together. Eight of us made our way to Bogue Chitto, Mississippi, to spend a week with the Choctaw Native Americans. I'll never forget this trip for a number of reasons, one of those being our devotions about the Fruit of the Spirit.

The organization tasked us with hosting a Bible School for the Choctaw youth, and we picked the theme "The Fruit of the Spirit." I can't say whether this had a lasting impact on any of the youth who attended, but I can say it made a profound difference in my own life.

Because of this study, I came to the realization that the Bible gave us a beautiful description of nine attributes that should be present – and bear fruit – in a believer's life: love, joy, peace, patience, kindness, goodness, faithfulness, gentleness, and self-control.

I truly desired to understand what this meant and thus started a multi-year, deep dive into the Fruit of the Spirit, studying the words in Greek, studying the concepts in Hebrew, exploring the Bible for descriptions of these attributes, reading what others had learned, and seeking to better understand this topic with an insatiable curiosity.

My studies resulted in an academic work that might be useful for a serious student or a pastor but would not appeal to most people. On the advice of my publisher, Mike Stickler, I began the journey of refashioning my studies into a fable that could put skin on these attributes and teach them in relatable and entertaining ways. I hope to accomplish this in *The Mentors Map Series*.

Most every character you will meet in this series reflects a composite of several people who have played a role in helping me grow to who I am today, and my continued maturity in the fruit of the Spirit. I chose many of my character's names as subtle winks to these men and women – letting them know how much they mean to me.

Now, let's get right to the story as we walk alongside Chuck Harper, who begins his journey of faith by learning about the Fruit of the Spirit.

PROLOGUE

In *The Mentors Map Series* you'll meet Chuck Harper, a young husband and father who seemingly has it all. As a hard-driving man, Chuck works in a fast-paced, high-pressure job that pays well. He has three great children and a lovely, supportive wife. Yet, while Chuck knows *something* is missing in his character, he does not know what that "something" might be.

In this first book of *The Mentor's Map Series*, Chuck begins to learn about that missing piece of his life. One Sunday morning, a reluctant decision initiates a life change Chuck never expected.

Each of these books delve into a mentoring journey around the Fruit of the Spirit, and each is meant to stand on its own. *Love, The Greatest of These* kicks off this series, and I welcome you to join me throughout the rest of the nine-book series as they are released.

Come with me now, and let's follow along as Chuck begins to learn about the Fruit of the Spirit and the attribute of Love.

A JADED VIEW

Is that a white hair? I'd just finished brushing my teeth and leaned in to take a closer look as Beth walked behind me to her sink. *My dear Beth, as beautiful as ever.* I thought, admiring her porcelain skin and strawberry blonde hair. I was still smitten.

"What are you looking at, handsome?" Beth teased.

"I thought I noticed a white hair," I replied.

"Honey, salt and pepper hair would suit you so well!"

Walking back into the bedroom, I took off my Rolex and sat on the edge of the bed. Beth sat down on her side of the bed and turned to me. "Let's go to church tomorrow."

Lately, she'd been putting on some pressure, telling me how we need to raise our kids in church.

"Okay, for you I'll go," I agreed reluctantly. "But don't you think a trip to the lake would be more fun?"

"Oh sweetie, thank you! We can go to the lake afterward if you really want to." As she turned out the lights, she reminded me, "Be sure I'm up by 8 o'clock so we can be on time."

I usually fall asleep quickly, but not tonight. I stared at the ceiling, thinking about church. I had grown up in church and remember as a kid that I just wanted to be a good person. Mom always told me that in kids' church we'd sing "I'm in the Lord's Army," and I would always shout out, "YES SIR!" louder than the other kids.

As with most kids, my enthusiasm waned as I entered my teens. Only after beginning college did I start viewing the world with a cynical and jaded eye. I wanted to be rich, and I didn't know any nice guys who ever got rich.

While I enjoyed some brotherhood with my college friends, in the end we all knew everyone was out for themselves, including us.

Because I was thriving professionally, I assumed my success was due to "looking out for Number One." Yet I longed for the lost innocence of a time when I believed people cared for and about one another. Maybe even a world where someone might do something for someone else just because it was the right thing to do – without expecting a personal benefit. Selflessness? Now that was a new concept.

I came to the same conclusion as always while dwelling on religion. *The church's teachings are more fantasy than reality.* I thought. *This is a dog-eat-dog world where self-preservation is a must to survive.* Settling that question for the time being, I pulled my mind off the Hamster wheel and went to sleep.

I woke up early on Sunday, as I do every day. I made a cup of coffee and walked through the living room to my study in the back corner of the house. I followed my usual routine of reading the news.

A pharmacy had been hit with a ransomware attack. While this was a bad day for someone, it was good for my business. A quick search revealed they were owned by a medical center that I had nearly won over as a client. Too bad for them. If they had signed with us, we could have helped them avoid this attack. I quickly fired off an email to the Chief Information Security Officer (CISO) of the medical center offering our recovery services.

I then noticed the time on my computer – it was already 8:07. I hurried back into the bedroom to wake Beth to find her already taking a shower, so I dashed upstairs to wake the kids. I found our seven-year-old, towheaded twins, David and Joseph, already playing a videogame, and our four-year-old baby girl, Abigail, watching a video on her iPad. They all took after their mother, but Abby especially was the spitting image of her mama.

"Hey guys, time to put down your games and videos and get dressed. Mom set out your clothes," I pointed toward their closet. "She'll be up to check on you soon."

I hurried back downstairs and across the house to my study. Just as I sat down, my phone rang. It was Walter, one of my coworkers.

"Did you see the news about the ransomware attack!" He launched in. "That pharmacy is owned by HBH Medical Center! I bet those idiots wished they hadn't walked away from the deal now!" The smugness in his voice was as thick as syrup.

After telling him I had already sent their CISO an email, he laughed and said, "If he replies, stick it to 'em!"

I knew this was an opportunity to make some good money, and even though this would cost them a fortune, they'd probably be a great reference after we got them out of this bind.

Since we started at Southside Consulting, Walter and I had struck up a friendship. We had made the company a fortune by taking advantage of every opportunity. The cybersecurity market was hot! And we were one of the fastest growing cybersecurity firms in the world. While we outsourced most of the technical work, the design all happened in house.

We had both recently been promoted to partners with the firm, largely because of our keen ability to find companies with money who had just been kicked in the face. We shrewdly took advantage of every opportunity with haste. Cybersecurity was always expensive, but much more so when you thought you might be down for the count, and this made us highly profitable.

Time had gotten away from me, and I hurried back to the bedroom to get dressed. I began buttoning up my crisp, white, dress shirt. Beth ran her hand across my back, purring as she walked by. She always said she loved a sharply dressed man. I decided to dress down a bit and not wear a tie, but I did wear one of my favorite navy suits.

As I rose from tying the laces of my two-tone brogue shoes, Beth came into view wearing a gorgeous light blue and white summer dress that brushed her ankles. The strap around her neck showed off her toned shoulders, and the sun coming in the window illuminated her like an angel. I could have just continued to stare at her, but the moment abruptly ended as she reminded me, "We're going to be late if we don't leave!"

"David, Joseph, Abby! Time to go!" I hollered up the stairs as I walked to the garage. Even though we took Beth's Escalade, I naturally hopped in the driver's seat. Because of its size, she never seemed to mind. Beth had wanted a smaller SUV, but I thought the Escalade fit our lifestyle better.

Before we made it out of the driveway, it started with Joseph. "David pinched me!"

"David, stop it!" I yelled.

"It wasn't me, Dad! He took my game!"

Then Abigail started screaming at the top of her lungs. Beth's tranquil beauty turned into fury as her face flushed. "Shut up, Abby! And quit it, boys!"

I couldn't help but notice the contrast between the peaceful yards in our subdivision and the havoc that filled the SUV. I tried to smile as I waved at Mrs. Johnson watering her flower bed.

We were nearing the church, but the chaos was growing. The boys were picking at each other, and Abby was still screaming. Beth unbuckled her seat belt and turned around, "If you don't stop now, I'm grounding you all!"

I looked at Beth in frustration, wondering why we were doing this to ourselves. In my most stern voice I yelled, "BEHAVE!" Finally, everyone quieted down as we pulled into the parking lot, though Joseph and Abby were both crying.

Beth got out of the car and vigorously wiped away their tears, telling them to both put on a smile. I let David out of the backseat on my side. We all pulled ourselves together and entered the church looking somewhat civilized.

When we walked in, a man I vaguely remember seeing welcomed us. "Hi Chuck and Beth! It's good to see you again!" he said.

I was thankful he had a nametag. Shaking his hand, I smiled and looked him in the eyes, "It's nice to see you too, Don." I couldn't help but notice his clip-on polyester tie and his well-worn sportscoat.

As he pointed off to the left, he reminded us that children's church was going on in the gym; Beth thanked him as she headed that way.

The church had three sections of seats. I was glad to see the ones we sat in years before were still open – three rows from the back on the right. The pews were gone though, and now they had modern-looking burgundy chairs.

An older couple in their 70s, Charles and Millie, sat in front of us and turned around to welcome me to the church. They obviously did not recognize me. Charles stuck his hand out, and I only then remembered his missing little finger. He had a very strong handshake. He must have worked with his hands. Millie was tiny compared to him; her black curled hair and thick glasses reminded me of a school librarian.

Right as the worship team started playing, Beth walked in and sat down beside me. In a snarky tone I said, "Aren't you glad we came to church?" Her furrowed eyebrows and pursed lips told me she wasn't amused.

RECONSIDERING LIFE

To my surprise, Pastor Ken was not preaching, making me wish even more that I had stayed home. They introduced the guest speaker, John, as a member of the church, though I didn't recognize him. He must have been in his seventies, though he looked healthy. He was shorter than average with hair as white as snow, which contrasted with his olive-toned skin.

John opened by saying, "The title of my message today is 'Bearing Fruit.'"

"Great," I whispered to Beth. "This is going to be a typical, Sunday, feel-good message that won't translate at all to the real world."

Beth looked at me with an annoyance that said, *You should just keep your mouth shut.*

Once John started teaching, however, I found myself engrossed in his message. He had an air of confidence and serenity about him. I could close my eyes and appreciate his voice – smooth and deep enough to narrate books or stories. This guy wasn't just preaching, he told genuine stories, as though he actually lived out what he said. He kept referring to "The Fruit of the Spirit" from Galatians 5:22-23.

"But the fruit of the Spirit is love, joy, peace, patience, kindness, goodness, faithfulness, gentleness, self-control. Against such things there is no law."

John shared compelling stories about interacting with others, causing me to think about my life. While I treated Beth and the kids "good" most of the time, I also showed my true colors at home on occasion. Even so, Beth wouldn't recognize me at work. I didn't earn the nickname "The Red Giant" for my patience and kind words. Just last Friday I lost my temper with Sandy, my assistant, because she bought dark instead of light-roast coffee.

Work at Southside is intense and fast-paced. Walter always tells the new grunts, "The pressure squeezes success out of winners and excuses out of losers!"

We hire intelligent, tough people who can handle the stress. We punish mistakes brutally, and often belittle and berate everyone. But it pays off. Our firm is growing, and anyone who stays long enough to get on an incentive plan makes good money.

John began wrapping up his sermon. "I'm going to ask some representatives from the men's group Noble Bereans to come to the front. If this message has spoken to you today, if you are feeling led to make a commitment to demonstrate a more Spirit-centered life, these men will be happy to talk with you."

I felt more pressure in my spirit than I had since I accepted Jesus when I was a child. No one in my professional life would call me a good person, but I hadn't always been that way. When I was young, I always wanted people to be happy, and I went out of my way to be nice, especially to adults. But that didn't pay in the real world, and a part of me longed for things to be different. What John was describing – a life filled with love, joy, peace and more – sure seemed better than what I had in my life now.

As we stood there, I sat my Bible down on the seat behind me and took half a step toward walking out into the aisle; but instead, I pulled back, hoping no one would notice.

After all, if it weren't for my style and forcefulness, we wouldn't have all these things we have now – the house, the car, the clothes, the toys, and the vacations.

My eyes darted back and forth to see who was watching. *Should I step out? I wanted more out of life, didn't I? Yes, of course. Wait, no, I can't do that.*

What if someone here knows me? What will they think? I debated with myself for what seemed like minutes, but in the end, I didn't allow myself to give in. It would be so embarrassing for others to see me walking forward, as if there were something wrong with me. I continued to wrestle with these feelings until John left the stage.

Beth whispered, "I'm going to get the kids," as she slipped past me out into the aisle. I stood there a moment longer before deciding to escape both the church and my feelings. As I made a beeline to the door, a man stopped me. "Chuck! You may not remember me; I'm Barry."

I did recognize him. It wasn't often I looked up to people, being over six-feet tall, but Barry actually looked down to talk to me at six-foot-four. From the looks of his suit and the sharp manner of his tie, I summed him up as a successful professional. He must have been about my dad's age, maybe in his late 50s, but he looked fit, like he took good care of himself. His hair was black, with a small bit of grey.

Barry placed his left hand on my shoulder, and we shook hands. He had a confident, firm handshake, and commanding presence. *What line of business is he in?* I wondered.

"We've talked before," Barry continued. "I noticed a moment ago you were considering going up front. I'm a member of Noble Bereans, the group John spoke about, and I'd love to take you out for breakfast one day this week. Maybe we could talk about it there?"

Great! I thought to myself with sarcasm as thick as honey. *They even set a trap in the back of the room!*

I didn't want to commit, but I didn't know how to say no. I could see the black Escalade straight out the door. If I could just get away, I'd be safely there in no time.

I quickly came up with an excuse, "I'm really busy this week. I'm sorry, I just—."

Not letting go of my hand and looking me *straight* in the eyes, Barry replied, "Well, let's make it shorter then and just have coffee. How's Tuesday at 7 work for you? The Uncommon Brew is a great coffee shop near the Interstate, and it should be convenient for you."

The trap door slammed shut, and I was caught. He must be in sales! Not seeing a way out, I hesitantly agreed.

Barry patted me on the shoulder and winked as he walked away saying, "I look forward to it!"

As I walked out of the building, it dawned on me that I had no idea how to contact him. No doubt, he planned this detail. How could I cancel if I couldn't call him? I turned around to ask for his number, but he was already talking with someone else. I turned back around and headed to the Escalade.

On the drive home, the kids were mostly quiet, playing with trinkets they had picked up in children's church.

Beth reached over and held my hand, smiling at me. "You seemed interested in the message today."

I didn't really want to show my feelings yet, so I said, "I thought John seemed genuine. He's either a great actor or a good person." I paused for a moment. "A guy caught me on the way out. A businessman of some sort. We're going to have coffee Tuesday."

"Oh?" Beth asked.

Not ready to admit that all Christians may not be alike, I simply replied, "Yeah."

A MEMORABLE COFFEE

Of course, when Tuesday morning came, everything in me wanted to cancel the meeting with Barry, but I didn't want to be a "no show." I resolved to be short and courteous over one cup of coffee, then make an excuse to be on my way.

Though I had passed by the coffee shop many times, I had never been to The Uncommon Brew before. Situated in a mostly deserted strip mall with heavily tinted windows, it didn't necessarily draw me in. Yet, when I walked through the door, the pleasant atmosphere surprised me with a delicious coffee aroma, well-spaced tables and chairs, and relaxed seating like a living room. The large fireplace in the corner added to the vibe and they had creatively decorated the walls with coffee art and logoed burlap bags. The soft jazz music and environment made it hard not to feel a bit more relaxed.

As I looked up at the menu board, I felt a hand on my back and Barry's baritone voice. "Come on, let's get a cup of coffee."

As we approached the counter, a dark-headed young lady said, "Will you have the usual, Mr. Kene?"

Barry replied, "Yes, Annie, and whatever Chuck wants too." I asked Barry what he usually ordered, and he replied, "A Brazilian light roast – black."

I was impressed. He at least knew about good coffee, and I loved a light roast. Turning to the young lady, I said, "I'll take the same."

As she handed us our coffee, Barry pointed to the comfy-looking blue armchairs situated near the fireplace with a small table between them. He led the way but offered to let me pick my seat.

"Let's begin with a word of prayer," Barry said, after taking his seat. This surprised me a bit and just as I started to bow my head, I spotted Walter walking in.

Ugh. If there's anyone I don't want Barry to meet, it's Walter. I couldn't help myself from thinking this awful thought.

Though Walter was short, he was stocky and hard to miss, especially with hair that seemed a little too blonde. He spent nearly every night after work at the gym. The only thing he talked about more than his physique was his ability to close deals. In fact, he had a dated-looking nameplate on his desk that simply said, "I CLOSE."

Even though he was my closest friend, we rarely did anything together outside of work, mostly because he made Beth feel uncomfortable around him. He was a player, and always showing up with a different woman, even interns from the firm. And while I could put on a different hat at work and at home, Walter was always aggressive and even abrasive.

I closed my eyes before he spotted me, hoping I would become invisible in the moment. Soon Barry said "Amen," the only word I heard.

Opening my eyes, I saw Walter walking toward me, with his loud voice disrupting the calm of the coffee shop. "Hey big guy! I've never seen you here before! I hope you and the preacher were just praying about that deal you need to close today!" He slapped me on the shoulder and, as he turned to walk out, he pointed at me and made this annoying double-clicking sound with his mouth. "I'll see you this afternoon!"

Now, I was so distracted I could hardly pay attention. Barry asked, "Co-worker?"

"Yeah, that was Walter Davidson. We're both partners at Southside Consulting."

"Oh! I've heard about Southside! You guys are really growing!"

"We are. Since Walter and I came on board we've multiplied the business several times. We're growing fast, and we're already one of the most respected names in cybersecurity consulting; before long we'll be the biggest too."

"I'm also in consulting," Barry replied. "I own Kene Business Advisors, though it won't be long until I start to phase into retirement. Dona and I have been married for 35 years, and we have five children: four boys, and a girl, and soon our fourth grandchild will be born! He's due in in just a few weeks on August seventh! How about you? Tell me a bit about your family."

"Beth and I have been married for almost eight years. We married when I was a sophomore in college. She's a part-time substitute teacher. We have twin boys who are seven, and we have a four-year-old girl." I chuckled a bit as I added, "No grandkids yet."

Barry smiled as he asked, "What did you think of the sermon Sunday?"

I set down my cup of coffee, then leaned back in my seat, locking my fingers together in front of me. "Well, honestly, I don't see anyone really living that way in my life, but when I heard John describing the Fruit of the Spirit, it sounded idyllic, and made me wish there really was a place where people lived that way. I love my job, and I'm good at what I do, but I don't want to live that way forever. If there were a country like he described, I think people would give up everything to live there. I know I would."

"There is a place like that. It's greater than any country; it's a Kingdom. Unfortunately, many people aren't willing to give up everything for it though. The world operates differently than the Kingdom, and most haven't reached a point where they can see something greater than this world. But, for those who really want it, for those who are willing to pursue it, the Kingdom is right here before them."

I looked up, a bit in disbelief. "No offense, but I don't see anyone living this way.

"Chuck, no one can live this way if they aren't pursuing God. I think you know who God is, but I don't think you really know God yet."

Defensively, I interrupted, "I got saved at a church camp when I was twelve!"

Barry's eyes tightened into a serious look. "Is there anyone in your life that you knew when you were twelve, but you lost contact with them, or you now only see them once in a while?"

"Yeah, I had a best friend in grade school that moved off." I thought about what I was saying before continuing, "We haven't spoken much since then, and we really don't have a lot in common now."

"What changed?" he asked.

"Well, I guess we just drifted apart."

Barry's blue eyes seemed to pierce into my soul as his eyes connected with mine. "Have you drifted apart from God?"

Before I thought about what I was saying, I answered, "I'm not sure I ever was close enough to God to drift apart."

"Chuck, I've been attending church for as long as I can remember, but several years ago I realized my life was not right. Church seemed dead to me; it was just a routine."

Barry leaned toward me, "I began studying the Bible on my own – a lot – and I realized there is more to this world than I thought. I began to realize that a Believer should reflect Jesus like a mirror, something I was not doing."

His eyes began to water, and his voice softened. "I felt shame about my business dealings, where all things were not honorable. I was taking advantage of people to make more money. And, if I'm honest, I wasn't being a good husband or father either. Inside I knew I believed in God, but that wasn't what I was showing the world."

The corners of Barry's mouth turned up as his somberness softened. "I met John at a fundraising event, and somehow our discussion turned to God. I still look back on that time as something orchestrated by God Himself. I had a discussion with John much like the one we are having now."

Barry took a sip of his coffee and gazed toward the windows before going on. "He then asked me a question I'll never forget. 'If you were on trial for being a Christian, would there be enough evidence to convict you?' I knew the answer to that question. I think that all of my studies prior to that moment helped prepare the ground, but it was *that day* when the real growth began."

Touched by this, I looked at Barry and said, "I want to grow too."

With a serious look Barry then said, "Chuck, you must understand what you're saying. The world will never be the same." His eyes connected with mine, then he asked, "Are you really ready for that? Before you answer, hear me out. You are going to be challenged in ways you cannot imagine. You are going to see your own weaknesses in ways you have never seen them before. And, as much as I wish this weren't true, you are almost certainly going to make big mistakes. But if you're ready for this, and I believe you are, then today your life will change forever."

I looked down at my cup of coffee as I thought through what Barry just said, and then lifted my head and replied, "I'm ready."

Barry smiled as he replied, "I knew you were!"

"Barry, can I ask a question? You mentioned John. What is his Noble Bereans group about?"

"Good question!" Barry enthusiastically said. "The name comes from the Noble Bereans in Acts 17:11. They were said to be noble minded and enthusiastic about receiving the gospel from Paul, but they didn't just accept what he said, they examined the Scriptures to see if it was true. That's our model – we don't just listen, but we study too, making sure what we hear and read is true."

Barry then picked up his cup of coffee and finished it off. Still holding his cup, he continued, "John started the group to help men live lives that honor the Lord and represent the Kingdom well. It's part accountability, part teaching, part debate, and solidly Christian. The real goal is to help men live their lives every day in a way that honors the King."

This King and Kingdom talk was a bit new and confusing to me, but I knew he was referring to God. I just wasn't accustomed to thinking of God as a King. Even so, I liked what he was saying.

Barry reached over and picked my empty coffee cup off the table, then he took both of our cups to the tray in the corner of the room. I suddenly felt like this meeting was over, but I wasn't ready for that!

I stood up just as Barry came back, and as he shook my hand, he said, "Chuck, we'll meet back here again next week. You have an assignment, though. I'd like to know what you think love is."

He continued, "Also, you might want to get a notebook to keep notes in. You're going to be learning a lot over the coming weeks." I then noticed the leatherbound notebook Barry had in his hand. He spotted me looking at it.

"Yes, that's my notebook. Any notebook will do, but I chose this one to make it special. You'll get to see a lot of this notebook. I carry it every time I'm planning on digging into the Word of God."

Barry then put his arm across my shoulder, and we walked out. As we left the building, he paused and said, "Father, bless this man today, and grant him favor as he begins to seek you out."

He then reached into his shirt pocket and pulled out a crisp, white business card. He turned it over and wrote 1 John 4:8 and Galatians 5:14 on the back, saying, "Start here." As he handed the card to me, he told me I could call him any time. He patted me on the shoulder as he walked toward a dark blue GMC pickup.

THE FIRST TEST

I arrived at work and settled in at my desk in the corner office. All through-out the day I found my mind reflecting on the conversation with Barry. At 2:00 I walked into the large conference room for a meeting. Before I'd even set down my laptop and coffee, Walter blurted out in front of everyone, "Chuck found religion this morning with a preacher man! Let's hope their prayers help him close this deal!"

Are you kidding me! I thought, as a tumult of emotions hit me and everyone laughed – everyone except Susie, a senior analyst on my team. Susie did not appreciate office games or digs like this.

Susie interjected, "Stop it, Walter. We have bigger things to focus on here."

After Susie's admonishment, the laughs died down quickly, allowing us to focus on the deal.

My head was not in the game though. The whole time I kept thinking about Walter's jeering and worrying I would see him again next week. For a moment I wondered if Barry could meet at another time. It was then I realized this might very well be my first test, and I decided to try and let it go.

Beth met me as I walked into our house that evening. "How was your day, honey?"

I kissed her on the forehead and said, "Just trying to close a deal." I then fixed up a plate of food from the dinner Beth had prepared and headed toward my study.

"Are you missing supper to work again?" she asked.

"I've got a lot going on," I replied.

I walked into the study and shut the door to hold down the distractions from Beth and the kids. I sat my food down on the desk, and then rolled down the shades to keep out the evening sun. When I sat back down, I noticed a note from Abby written in crayon peeking out from under my plate, "I love you daddy!" I pinned it on the corkboard behind me, then began looking for my Bible. I soon realized it was still in Beth's Escalade in the garage. Rather than face more questions from her, I searched for an online Bible, and, as I ate, I looked up the verses Barry wrote on the back of the card:

---

*1 John 4:8 "The one who does not love does not know God,
because God is love."*

---

*Galatians 5:14 "For the whole law is fulfilled in one statement,
namely, "You shall love your neighbor as yourself."*

The first verse he wrote down said, "God is love." *Is this what he was looking for?* After reading the second verse, I didn't think so. It said, "love your neighbor as yourself." I re-read the first verse, and it hit me! *If we aren't loving others like we love ourselves, then we do not know God!*

I set my fork down on the plate and thought of all the ways I showed love to Beth and the kids – our house, the cars, the vacations, the private schools. But the more I thought about it, the more bothered I became. We went on vacation to the beach because I loved the beach. Beth often mentioned other places. Beth had also wanted to live in the country where she could have a horse, but I chose the new subdivision because of the prestige. Everything I could think of was an example of how I got my way, not how I had shown love to Beth or the kids. I then realized that I had just blown her off after she had fixed supper for the family.

I was worse at this than I thought! I picked up my plate and headed back to the dining room. The boys were nearly done eating, and Abby was playing with her food. Beth didn't say anything at first, and I could tell she was not happy. I decided to focus on Abby for a minute to break the silence.

"Abby?"

She looked at me with a smile and enthusiastically asked, "Yes, daddy?"

I replied, "Thank you for the sweet note, baby girl."

Abby's smile stretched even wider across her face. I could see Beth looking at her, but she didn't break her stoic silence.

David asked, "May we be excused?"

Beth nodded her head, and the boys both grabbed their plates and headed back to the kitchen. Abby followed right behind them.

Beth and I finished supper in silence, then, as we were almost done, I said, "I'm sorry, Beth."

"It's okay. I just wish you'd eat with us more often. You work long hours already, then you come home and go right to your study to work more."

"I understand," I replied. I got up and walked behind her, wrapping my arms around her as I kissed her on the top of her head. "Please forgive me."

As I unwrapped my arms, Beth stood up and said, "You're forgiven." She then smirked as she continued, "Just don't let it happen again!"

After supper, I made my way back to the study and re-read the verses Barry had given me. I then tried to think of ways to show love. *Maybe I could host a dinner party for our neighbors.* I decided to think about it before telling Beth. I scribbled it on a sticky note.

That reminded me about the notebook. I didn't have one, but while it was on my mind I searched online and found one like Barry's. I liked the idea of making it special. In the meantime, I took notes of what I had discovered in my studies on my computer.

I read more in the Bible that evening and throughout the week, and every time I saw the word "love," my eyes lit up. I began to realize how much the Bible talks about love! I searched online and found lots of verses talking about love! I found out that 1 Corinthians 13 was also known as the love chapter. And as I read on, I saw in 1 Corinthians 16:14 that all our actions should be done with love. I put that in my notes. Then, in 1 Peter 4:8, I read that, "love covers a large number of sins." I thought about that for a minute, not understanding what it meant, but I wrote it down anyhow.

I hadn't really told Beth much about what was going on except that I had met with Barry for coffee, and she certainly didn't know I had been reading the Bible at night. I had such apprehension about admitting I might need to change my way of thinking.

Saturday night, as I prepared for bed, I asked, "Would you like to go to church again tomorrow?"

Surprised, Beth asked, "Sure. Is everything okay?"

"I enjoyed it last week, and I thought I could introduce you to Barry," I replied.

The following morning, I made sure to be ready on time but the drive to church did not differ much from last week. I wondered how kids could fight so much over such a short distance.

When we walked into the church, I was surprised to see Barry standing with Don at the door. I had a hard time ignoring the contrast in their attire as well as their height. Barry eagerly reached out his hand to welcome me with a firm handshake. He turned to Beth and said, "Hi Beth. We've met before, but it's been a long time. Welcome."

Beth politely replied and we both shook hands with Don too. Beth then excused herself to take the kids to Children's Church.

"Barry, thanks for inviting me last week," I said. "I've been reading the Bible this week, and I'm looking forward to our coffee again on Tuesday."

He smiled and replied, "Me too."

A few minutes later I found my seat and the music started playing. Beth arrived back from dropping off the kids. As she sat down, she said, "Barry seems nice."

"I really like him, and I think you will too," I said.

After the service I noticed Barry in earnest discussion with someone else, though we exchanged a brief wave as I walked out.

That evening I studied more on love, and I found a part of the Bible that surprised me – the *Song of Solomon!* I never realized the Bible had a book on romance! I chuckled a bit at my discovery, but I moved on thinking this wasn't what Barry had in mind in our study on love.

THE FIRST BIG STUMBLE

Tuesday morning a pop-up thunderstorm struck just as I arrived at The Uncommon Brew. I pulled in right next to Barry, who had arrived just before me. We got out of our cars and hurriedly walked in together under a downpour.

We took the same seats as last week, and Barry asked to pray before our discussion. What a relief *not* to see Walter this time! After praying, Barry asked, "What have you learned about love?"

"I've seen the word a lot as I read the Bible this week, but from the two verses you shared, I think we should be showing love to others if we truly love God," I replied.

"But what does that mean?" Barry asked. "How do you show love to others?"

"We should treat others like we want to be treated," I said.

He smiled, "You're getting there."

Barry savored his coffee for a moment. "Chuck, you mentioned that you'd seen the word 'love' in the Bible. In the New Testament there are three Greek root words used for love. The first is phileō. You might recognize this."

"Is that the root word for Philadelphia – the city of brotherly love?" I asked.

"That's really a good definition of that word," Barry replied. "It refers to close friendship.

"The second word is storgē, which is used to describe a family-like affection. This root word isn't even used in the New Testament, only variations of the word."

I smiled as this made me think about how good it made me feel for Abby to leave me a note in my office this week. My smile faded as I thought back to the other lesson I had learned that same night about my love for my family.

Barry continued, "Finally, we get to the one that matters most for our discussion: agapē. This is the root word used in the verses I gave you. This is also the word used for love in Galatians 5, about the fruit of the Spirit."

Barry took another sip of coffee before continuing. "I once heard agapē defined as 'a God kind of love,' and maybe that's because it's primarily found in the Bible. I like that definition, but it doesn't tell us a lot. Broadly speaking, the actual definition could be a couple of things.

"First, it could mean a shared fellowship meal. But for our purposes, it's the other definition that matters. It's having genuine regard for and interest in others. You could even call it affectionately caring for others."

Eager to show I was paying attention, I responded, "Affection makes it sound like family, like I have affection toward Beth. How's that differ from the other word you mentioned – storey –?"

"Storgē," Barry replied. "Think of storgē as that special affection you feel toward family. Think of agapē as a genuine love and concern for others. Remember, it's not just our family we should have this genuine regard for."

"That makes sense, thanks," I replied.

"Don't worry, we're going to explore this more over the coming weeks," he said. "It shouldn't surprise you that I'm going to give you another assignment though."

I smiled affirmingly as Barry continued, "This week I want you to dig more into the Greek word agapē. You can search online to find everywhere it's used in the Bible. Ask yourself what you can learn from its use."

"I look forward to diving into this! Do you have any recommendations on where to begin?" I asked.

Barry smiled again, "As a matter of fact, I do. Why don't you start your reading this week in First Corinthians 13?"

He picked up my empty coffee cup and placed both of our cups on the tray in the corner. I stood up, knowing our brief meeting was over. The rain had stopped, and we walked out together.

Just as we reached our vehicles, Barry turned to me and said, "Oh, one other thing, Chuck. Next week, why don't you share with me how you've exhibited love this week?"

As I drove to the office, I wondered where I might show love this week. *What about that dinner party for the neighbors? Nah, I probably couldn't do it this week. Perhaps I could do something for Beth and the kids?*

As I stopped at a red light, a man approached my car. His sign read, "Please help. Out of work. Roses $2, $20 a dozen." I'd seen these bums before, and I always avoided making eye contact. I quickly drove once the light turned green. Then it hit me! I could have showed this man love by buying roses. He was trying to be productive in his situation. Not only would I be helping this man, but then I could have shown love to Beth by bringing her roses. A twofer! *If he's there later today, I'll buy a dozen roses.*

In ten minutes I arrived at the office, but the day went downhill from there. I didn't win the deal I had been working on, and we received an unexpected notice that another client would not be renewing their contract. That double-whammy put me in a foul mood. During our afternoon meeting, I lashed out at Marshall, one of the newer members of the team, for not making sure we had all the data we needed to win the deal.

After I finished the lashing, Walter sealed it with a quip, "Losers don't last. We keep the best and cull the rest."

As we dismissed the meeting and I walked back to my desk, Marshall approached me, "I'm sorry about that, sir. It's my first time looking at that kind of data, but it won't happen again."

I barely acknowledged him, "Just remember, losers don't last."

I ended up staying overtime trying to write the recap on why we lost this deal. When I left the office, the stormy weather picked up again. An accident on the Interstate delayed me even further, and by the time I made it home, it was nearly the kids' bedtime. Beth tried to give me a hug, asking if it had been a tough day.

I halfway hugged her back. "I just need to wind down."

I sat in my recliner and stewed over the day's problems while Beth watched TV. Finally, having had enough of this day, I got up and said, "Goodnight."

Beth replied, "Tomorrow will be better."

It wasn't though. It soon became clear that I had made a mistake on this important deal. No one knew it but me, and I sure wasn't going to admit it.

On Thursday everyone pulled a late night at the office trying to meet a proposal deadline. Most of the team worked in the conference room, snacking on a pizza, but I stayed in my office. One of the technical writers, Deb, came to let me know they had the proposal ready for my review. Once I completed the review, the team could go home.

I opened the document and noticed they'd used the wrong font. I stormed into the conference room. "You guys think it's okay to submit half-reviewed work because it's evening? You used the wrong font, which means you didn't even look this over! Look on the wall! Do you think I got all these awards for being lazy? No, I got these awards because I'm the best, and when you're the best, you don't miss things like this!"

I continued, "No one leaves until you've reviewed your section again. No mistakes! Let me know when it's ready for my review." I walked out of the conference room in a huff.

A half hour later Deb came back to my office, letting me know they'd reviewed the sections and were ready for approval – with no changes except the font. I could feel my face turning red and the rage boiling up inside of me.

"But it clearly has not been reviewed! Are you sure it's ready?"

"Yes, sir. We're sure."

After going over the proposal with a fine-tooth comb, I found two small errors, and the team corrected them quickly. Then after my approval, Susie came by my office and asked, "How about letting the team come in a couple of hours later tomorrow? It's been a long day."

I was still furious about their carelessness, and I wasn't about to let Walter get ahead this quarter. Without looking up, I replied, "I'll be here at eight tomorrow."

Friday afternoon I saw a press release that a competitor had helped HBH Medical Center successfully navigate their ransomware attack. I didn't really expect the job, since they never replied to my initial email and phone calls, but I didn't expect to lose the work to another full-service firm like us. It was a fitting way to end an already bad week.

Sunday rolled around, and Beth asked if we were going to go to church again. I replied, "No, I'm just not into it today."

It was then I realized I hadn't read a thing in the Bible this week, and I sure wasn't ready for coffee with Barry on Tuesday. For a fleeting moment I had a twinge of regret, but quickly reasoned it away with a grunt. *Who am I fooling? This is just fantasy versus reality.*

"Okay," Beth replied with concern in her voice. "I just thought you seemed like you were happy going last week. Maybe next week?"

"Maybe," I answered coolly.

Monday evening, Barry texted me, "I missed you at church on Sunday. I look forward to seeing you tomorrow."

I replied, "Sorry, Barry. Busy week. Maybe next week."

Barry replied, "How can I help?"

I didn't reply right away, not knowing how to respond.

AUGUST REFOCUSED

One week of missing church and coffee turned into two, until I found a package in my study when I arrived home one Thursday. It was the notebook I had ordered!

I put the three notepads into the leather notebook and then closed it. It really felt special. I opened it back up and decided to move the notes I had taken on my computer to the notebook. Reading through them and writing them down made me slow down and realize how far I had fallen from just a few weeks ago.

I had missed opportunity after opportunity to show love to others. I could have supported the needy man selling roses. I could have shown love to Beth multiple times. I could have avoided taking advantage of Marshall when the deal fell through. And I could have admitted my fault later. Not only that, but the way I reacted to the team's mistake was uncalled for and rude.

As soon as I finished thinking this through, I texted Barry. "Sorry I've missed our coffees. Can we meet next week?"

Barry replied, "Yes, and I'll see you Sunday too?"

I had to think about that. I was not feeling it, but I knew I needed to be there for myself. "Yes, I'll be there."

I opened the desktop app I had found to read the Bible. It seemed like this version was easier to understand than my Bible. But I realized I had not written down the verse Barry had referred to a few weeks ago, and I couldn't remember the reference. I didn't want to admit that to him, so I wrestled with myself, trying to pull it out of the recesses of my mind. I did remember I was supposed to read about agapē though, so I began by searching for "agape" on the Internet along with "bible verses." I found several examples, and one of them rang a bell: 1 Corinthians 13! That was it! Relieved, I immediately pulled it up on my computer and, just as quickly, realized why he had pointed me here.

---

1 Corinthians 13:3b-8 "… but [if I] do not have love, it benefits me nothing. [4] "Love is patient, love is kind, love is not jealous, it does not boast, it does not become conceited, [5] it does not behave dishonorably, it is not selfish, it does not become angry, it does not keep a record of wrongs, [6] it does not rejoice at unrighteousness, but rejoices with the truth, [7] bears all things, believes all things, hopes all things, endures all things. [8]"Love never ends."

I buried my head in my hands, "Why, God, why? Why did You let me mess up?"

I thought about how cruel I had been to Marshall and the other folks at work. The incident with Marshall almost haunted me. I had verbally assaulted him. Though he had made a mistake, it was really my mistake that lost the contract, but he was crucified in my place. My life seemed like a great example of the opposite of the Fruit of the Spirit. I leaned my head back and looked at the ceiling as I said out loud, "Please help me, God! Please!"

After regaining my composure, I wrote down this passage in my new notebook. I then turned back to the computer and tried to make up for my failures by sending an email thanking the team at Southside for all their hard work. As I was typing I realized I had never done something like this.

I couldn't help but wonder who would be the first to thank me tomorrow. With this, I decided to go to bed on a positive note.

I left for work early on Friday, and by midday, I was surprised that no one brought up the email I sent last night. I finally asked Deb if she received it.

"Yeah, that was kind of weird," she replied.

Was I really so bad that a complimentary email was weird? Unfortunately, I knew the answer.

Soon, Sunday rolled around, and though I resisted, I put on a smile, and we all went to church. I was glad I went. The worship team performed a song called "My Jesus, My Savior." The words of the song were so powerful that I even began crying as I quietly sang along.

Brother Ken also had another good message about what it means to serve God that left me thoughtful about my relationship with the Lord. I didn't see Barry before the service, but afterward, I saw him walking up with a woman. He introduced her to Beth and me as his wife, Dona.

Dona reminded me of an older version of Beth, even the smile. Whereas Beth was more reserved, Dona was exuberant, hugging us both as if she had known us her whole life. I was happy to see Dona and Beth connecting so well. In the few minutes we stood there, they knew more about each other than Barry and I had found out since we started meeting more than a month ago.

After a few minutes, Beth excused herself to go get the kids, and I went out to cool down the Escalade while waiting for Beth and the kids.

Beth had barely buckled her seatbelt when she said, "They are nice people! No wonder you like Barry so much."

I kiddingly replied, "Barry's who I want to be when I grow up!"

Beth playfully slapped me on the shoulder as she said, "Stop it, Chuck!"

Thankfully, the week started out quietly. We didn't lose any business, but I had hoped we might get good news from the proposal we submitted late last Thursday. Unfortunately, it was quiet on that front too.

While I had resisted going to church on Sunday, I really did look forward to seeing Barry on Tuesday. That was only tempered by my embarrassment of not having coffee with him for a few weeks.

When I arrived at the coffee shop early, I was surprised to see Barry already seated and talking with another man. He waved at me and told me my coffee was already paid for. As I approached Barry and this other man, they both stood up. I was a bit surprised. The other man looked like an industrial worker of some sort. He had on blue coveralls and work boots. Barry didn't seem to mind though, and said, "This is my friend, Dwayne. Dwayne, this is Chuck. Chuck, Dwayne has quite a story, one I think you'd like to hear sometime."

Dwayne and I shook hands. His handshake was quite firm, and his hand felt rough. I wondered what kind of work he did.

Dwayne politely excused himself, and I apologized for interrupting, though Barry shrugged it off as if it were nothing.

Annie walked up with my coffee, and as soon as Barry and I sat down, I started talking, my guilt leading the way.

"I'm sorry I've missed our coffees lately. It's not been a good few weeks." I then took a sip of my coffee to give my emotions a moment to catch up. "Last week I finally read First Corinthians 13 like you suggested, and I realized that I'm none of the things written there about love." I went on to tell him all that had happened and how it made me feel resistant to talk about God, even insufficient, as if this wasn't for me.

I could tell Barry was really listening, until I paused. We sat in the quiet of the coffee shop for a moment, and then Barry said, "Chuck, I am glad you came back. I was getting worried about you. I thought you were ready for this, but like I told you, it's not going to be easy. You are going to fail. More than once. You're human, after all. And believe me, there's nothing the enemy wants more than to keep you from growing in your walk with the Lord. If you're ready to listen and learn though, mistakes are often better teachers than success."

I hesitated. *How could I say what I wanted to say after these last few weeks?*

"Barry," I replied, "I am ready. I hope I don't mess up again, but I'm not a very good person, and I need a lot of work. Just don't give up on me."

Barry drank his coffee and thought for a moment. "The Bible tells us that none of us are good. Our human nature is sinful and broken, and we live in a broken world. We are all unworthy on our own, but we were made worthy by Jesus' sacrifice. As we grow in Him, the enemy will fight us with everything he has. He doesn't want us to grasp what is there for us. He certainly doesn't want us to understand love."

This certainly wasn't the motivational pep talk I was hoping for, but I also appreciated that Barry didn't sugarcoat anything. Something about this conversation made it more credible to me.

Barry continued, "When we started meeting, Chuck, we started out talking about love for a reason. Of all the virtues of a believer, love is the most important. Some even believe that love is the master virtue, and all the others are just derivatives of love. While you may exhibit some of the rest of the Fruit of the Spirit in your life now, you'll not really exhibit those characteristics in the strongest way unless you first have love."

"I never really knew that love was so complicated. There's a lot to it," I replied.

Barry nodded, then he pointed to my empty cup, "Refill?"

"Sure," I replied.

Barry soon returned with two fresh cups of coffee. He continued, "There's a lot to it, but it's not really complicated. Remember what we talked about last time from Galatians 5:14? That we should love our neighbors like we love ourselves? I think this is a good litmus test to see whether we are walking in love or not."

Barry took a sip of his coffee and seemed to be thinking about something. He then asked, "Do you know a foreign language?"

"Yes," I replied. "I know Spanish and a little Italian."

Barry continued, "When you are translating from Spanish or Italian to English, do you ever have trouble picking the right word?"

"Yeah," I answered, "Sometimes it takes a couple of words to really translate something."

Barry explained, "The Bible is no different. We often don't think about what it took to get the English Bible in our hands. The Old Testament was written in Biblical Hebrew. The New Testament is widely believed to have been written in Greek, though some believe it was written partially or totally in Aramaic, a Semitic language related to Biblical Hebrew. At a bare minimum we are translating from ancient Greek to English, but we are also dealing with underlying meanings only understood from a Semitic, cultural point of view. This is a long way of saying that just reading the Bible gives us an understanding of what is said, but studying the Bible can bring out a much deeper meaning than we first realized."

It took me a minute to absorb what Barry just said. "I thought you said it wasn't complicated?"

Barry chuckled. "Love is not complicated, but we can learn more about what it means if we really study it. And today we'll begin doing that."

Barry picked up his mug, and as he was about take a sip, he asked, "Would you mind reading First Corinthians 13:4-7?"

"Sure. Just give me a minute to find it." I picked up my phone and opened the Bible app. "Love is patient, love is kind, love is not jealous, it does not boast, it does not become conceited, it does not behave dishonorably, it is not selfish, it does not become angry, it does not keep a record of wrongs, it does not rejoice at unrighteousness, but rejoices with the truth, bears all things, believes all things, hopes all things, endures all things."

Leaning in, he lowered his voice and said, "If you say you love someone, you should exhibit these behaviors. After the last few weeks, I think you've seen how hard this is. It's not just our spouses or family members, but we should exhibit these behaviors toward our neighbors, our friends, and our brothers and sisters in Christ. It doesn't even stop there. What about the needy or those who are sometimes considered unlovable?"

That last statement really challenged me. I could see how we should love those close to us, and those we interact with, but I avoided the indigent, especially those who sat on the corner begging all day. *Was I really wrong about this?*

Barry broke my thought as he continued, "Patience is the first word there. I don't know about you, but I have always struggled with patience. This doesn't simply mean to wait patiently when someone is late. In Greek, this word conveys something much stronger than that. It means being patient even when someone pushes your buttons. In other words, patience means that you don't let someone else get to you and draw anger out of you. We're not going to explore this more today. Patience is one of the virtues listed in the Fruit of the Spirit, so you'll dive deeper into this later."

I quietly sighed in relief – knowing how much I would struggle with patience. Then it hit me, "Kindness is a Fruit of the Spirit too, right?"

Barry said, "You're right. Here, both words are verbs – think of action. In the Fruit of the Spirit, they are nouns, think of attributes. Just like in English though, there are some nuances. For example, the word used for kindness here in Galatians is not used anywhere else in the Bible. It is the action of being kind or loving, or even merciful. It could also refer to a willingness to help someone else. Here's the key though: this refers to acting rather than sitting idly by when someone needs help."

My mind immediately flashed back to the needy. *Was God trying to tell me something?* In a moment of reprieve, I remembered something I'd heard, then blurted it out, "The Bible says God helps those that help themselves, right?"

Barry answered, "No, that's not in the Bible. It's probably an ancient Greek proverb, but many attribute it to Ben Franklin. The Bible says just the opposite."

Barry opened his journal and thumbed through it. "Ah yes, here it is. Romans 5:6 says, 'For while we were still helpless, Christ died for us.' I suppose if He thought that much of the helpless, we should consider them too."

I quickly jotted that down in my notebook to research later.

Barry picked up my coffee cup, a sign that the lesson was over for the day. I stood up as he returned from the tray where he deposited the cups. As we walked out of the coffee shop, he stopped and turned toward me. Placing his hand on my shoulder he said, "Remember, you have more challenges ahead. I can count on you being here next week though, right?"

"Right. What should I study?"

Barry said, "Just keep reading about love. And re-read First Corinthians 13. We'll be on this topic for a bit." He then waved bye as he walked to his truck.

I felt like I had learned so much in these few minutes over coffee, and I resolved that I would not let these meetings slide again.

IT'S MY PARTY

Over the next week, I studied 1 Corinthians 13 and Galatians 5, trying to glean what I could. I spent time studying the Bible every night, especially paying attention to the two attributes or actions of love in 1 Corinthians 13: love is not jealous and does not boast. The word "boast" gave me a sick feeling.

Walter and I were the kings of trash talk and bragging. I thought about the time I threw a party to celebrate the firm's success, but I made sure to prominently display the award I had received at an industry gala. Everyone got the message that night loud and clear: the firm succeeded because I succeeded. It was all because of me!

Then I thought of the whole "wrong-font episode." As if that wasn't bad enough, I made sure Deb and every other employee on my team knew all about my greatness after their small mistake. I still remember pointing to my awards in the conference room and saying, "I got these awards because I'm the best!"

Throughout the week, I made a conscious effort *not* to talk *about myself*, but my tendency toward self-aggrandizement still controlled my tongue more than I cared to admit.

For our next study over coffee, Barry and I arrived near the same time. On the way into the coffee shop I asked him how he learned more about these Greek definitions."

"It will be easier to show you. Why don't you and Beth join us for lunch after church on Sunday?"

"That sounds great! I'm sure Beth will be happy too." Truthfully, I was looking forward to learning more, but I really wanted to see where Barry lived.

We ordered our coffee, and Barry prayed for God's guidance, which I always appreciated. We jumped right in to our study…just as Walter walked in the door. I wished I could somehow put my work life into a different box and not risk someone like Walter interfering.

After ordering his coffee to go, Walter walked by and patted me on the back as he looked at Barry and said, "Hey preacher man, did Chuck tell you how your prayers failed a few weeks ago? Maybe you didn't give enough offering!"

Barry stood up to introduce himself, but Walter had made sure to move quickly and was headed out the door.

Barry sat back down as he said, "Interesting guy."

I nodded, wishing he wasn't so offensive. I wasn't quite as brash as Walter, but I knew that could have just as easily been me in a different situation.

Barry asked, "Do you know what the next two descriptors of love are from First Corinthians 13?"

"Love is not jealous, and it does not boast," I replied.

"That's right. These two aren't too hard either. The translation I most often use, the ESV, states, 'Love does not envy or boast.' The NET version, a version I really like for the notes, states, 'Love is not envious. Love does not brag.' All three of these translations are stating this well."

I wasn't going to get away from this word boast. I knew this was going to be a challenge for me.

Barry continued, "Let's start with envy or jealousy, depending on your translation. Both work well here, but I think envy is probably the intent. Envy and jealousness are often used interchangeably, but jealousness is really describing a fear we have of someone being better than us. Envy is desiring what someone else has, which is why I think that's a better choice here. In fact, I think there is even a better word – one we don't use very often – the word 'covet.' The point here is that a person operating in love does not set their heart on someone else's things or their life, seeking to take what they have or even making themselves heartsick because they do not have it."

Barry took a sip of his coffee and let that sink in. This was certainly speaking to me. I had never thought about the difference between these two words, but now I realized I was full of both jealousy and envy. With embarrassment, I remembered how often I had said, *I want it all, and I want it now!* Worse yet, I didn't really want anyone else to have it. I wanted to be on top and stay on top.

Barry then explained further, "I think it goes a bit deeper though. Someone can exhibit envy or covetousness when they go overboard emulating someone else. You've seen this, I'm sure, where someone tries so much to be just like the person they admire that it goes beyond flattery, and you soon realize they truly want to be that person."

My mind immediately went to my car. I recently bought my Audi RS 7 because Mr. Barton, our CEO, had a very similar car when I started at the firm. I even bought the same color, black, because "that's what professionals drive."

"You look thoughtful," Barry said.

I replied, "I'm just thinking. I probably do some of this."

"I thought you might. Unfortunately, the world promotes this way of thinking."

I slowly nodded in agreement.

Barry continued, "Next we see that 'Love does not boast.' As I mentioned a moment ago, the NET version uses 'brag,' which I think also works here. I like how Webster's defines this: to heap praise on oneself. This is the person who just can't quit talking about how good they are. No one wants to be around this person, especially not for long."

Here we go. Everyone at work, and even in the industry, knew Walter and I were the best. We reminded them so often, we made sure they couldn't help but know it.

I thought back to that celebration dinner again. Walter and I had just come back from the industry gala, and I was itching to be sure everyone knew I had received a big award. I couldn't think of a tactful way to tell everyone at the office, so I set up a big party at the Country Club, even inviting everyone to bring someone. I announced that I wanted to 'celebrate our success,' but anyone could clearly see the purpose for this dinner. Who was I fooling? I displayed my award on the table beside the lectern, and just as I had hoped, Walter made a big deal of it too. In the end, the whole event turned out uncomfortable, and everyone realized it had nothing to do with the firm and was all about me.

Pulling out of my thoughts, I then noticed Barry kept quiet, waiting on me.

"Are you good for one more?" Barry asked.

"I didn't really study further, but let's do it," I replied.

Barry continued, "Love is not conceited—"

I interrupted, "Isn't this a lot like boasting?"

Barry replied, "They're similar, but different. Someone who is boasting doesn't always really believe what they are saying. Someone who is conceited, full of arrogance or pride, truly believes they are somehow better than everyone else. I think an even better word for this is 'haughty,' another word we don't use often. It's when someone looks down with contempt or disdain on others they think are inferior."

Worried about what I was hearing, I asked, "Like a superiority complex?"

Barry exclaimed, "Yes, Chuck, that's it!"

I knew I was boastful, but I hadn't really thought of myself as conceited. It just went from bad to worse though. I was haughty! *But was it haughty if it was true? The firm wouldn't be where it is without me. Mr. Barton even said as much.*

Walter and I had grown the company several times larger than he had been able to. There were winners in life, and there were losers too, right? *Should I hide that I'm a winner?*

My mind then wandered back to last week's coffee where I walked in on Barry and Dwayne talking. *What was a successful person like Barry doing with a person like him?* Barry seemed to be friends with him though. All this felt a bit like trying to see through fog. I knew there was something there, but I struggled to grasp it.

"You seem to be reflecting on this, Chuck. How about we break here for the week, and next week we'll continue? Oh, and don't forget lunch on Sunday. You can follow us to our place after church."

As Barry reached over to get my coffee cup, I picked it up and reached out for his. "Today I've got them." He smiled as he handed me his cup.

UNREALIZED
EXPECTATIONS

I found a Bible reading plan online and started reading it the next morning. In the evening, I wanted to study more about love. When I read the next phrase, "[love] does not behave dishonorably," I thought about one of the Ten Commandments, "Honor your father and your mother." I jotted that down. I also noticed a few passages referring to selfish ambition, and one of them was right before the Fruit of the Spirit in Galatians 5:20. I wrote that down too. I was really beginning to appreciate that I could easily go back and read through my earlier thoughts.

Though we'd had an eventful week at work, at least we didn't get any "bad news." On Friday afternoon we even closed a surprise deal, one I hadn't done much work on because I didn't think they could afford it. As I walked out and marked another win on the board. Instead of initialing it with my initials though, I wrote "A-Team," hoping everyone would see how I recognized the team instead of myself. I then announced it loudly and told everyone to take off early and enjoy the weekend.

Sunday morning, we took the kids to Beth's parents so we could enjoy some adult time with Barry and Dona. After church, Barry and Dona met us in the lobby and we followed them to their house.

We went in a different direction than I expected, toward an older part of town. We turned off the main road into an unfamiliar and older subdivision. It seemed quiet and clean, but I was a bit surprised. The modest ranch style homes from the 70s with modest cars in the driveways seemed very humble compared to what I'd pictured. When Barry's truck pulled into a driveway, I looked at Beth and said, "This isn't what I expected."

"What do you mean by that? It looks like a nice home," she replied.

And it was nice, but not fancy. It was a split-level made of dark-red brick. The tidy landscaping seemed pretty basic. I had really expected Barry to live somewhere more prestigious like Mr. Barton. I wondered if maybe his business wasn't doing as well as I thought.

As we walked in, Barry and Dona set their things down. I could see that Dona had already set the dining room table, and soon Barry and Dona were taking the food out of the oven and the refrigerator. Beth hopped right in, and I soon realized I was the only one standing there. I asked how I could help, and Barry asked me to put some ice in the glasses.

"Dona and I will take water. There are other drinks in the refrigerator. Feel free to get whatever you and Beth would like."

I found a Coke for Beth and sparkling water for myself. As I took the drinks to the table, Barry was setting down a pan of pot roast with potatoes and carrots. There were green peas, salad, and raw vegetables on the table. Dona walked in carrying Brown 'N Serve rolls.

I couldn't remember the last time I had eaten pot roast with potatoes and carrots. It smelled really good but reminded me of my parent's home growing up. It even felt sort of like mom and dad's house: a bit ordinary.

Barry said, "We had thought about hamburgers and hotdogs, but because it's so hot we decided against it. I hope we've cooked something you like."

Beth replied, "This looks delicious, thanks!"

Barry said, "Have a seat, then let's begin with prayer."

Barry's prayer was unlike any I had heard before a meal. I was accustomed to hearing rote prayers at the table, but Barry thoughtfully asked God to bless the food and our lives, especially as we seek to learn about Him and serve Him.

We had a nice conversation over lunch. While Dona and Beth continued to get along well, it surprised me how curious Barry and Dona were about our lives. They asked Beth and me a lot of questions and seemed to genuinely care about us.

After lunch, Barry asked me to come with him to his study, and Dona asked Beth to join her in the living room.

Barry pulled a folding chair out of the hall closet and brought it with him to the study, which looked like it had been originally designed as a bedroom. There was a nice desk and chair, a computer, bookshelves, and a couple of comfortable seats across from the desk. Barry handed the chair to me as he said, "I know this folding chair isn't as comfortable as the chairs on the other side of the desk, but it will be easier for me to show you how I study the Bible if you're sitting over here with me."

He sat down at his computer without grabbing a book, which surprised me. He motioned for me to unfold the chair and join him as he turned a monitor toward me.

"I love books, Chuck, but I've found for Bible study the computer is better for me. I still read a traditional Bible. There's nothing like holding a book in your hands! But when it comes to studying, I'm so much more efficient on the computer. My mentor, John, still likes to use books for everything though."

Soon he had a program pulled up on his computer – the same one I used, Logos Bible Software. I could see that he had a lot of books in his digital library though, and I only had a few. After opening a few things, he turned to me to explain, "I've found there are a few essential things to better understand the Bible, and then there are many more which will help you in deeper studies."

Over the next half hour, he gave me a lot of recommendations he called "tools" to help me dive deeper into Bible study. As we wrapped up, I reviewed my long list of notes. "This is a lot," I said.

"Remember, no one needs all this. They are just study helps. Just pick one tool and use it. You'll know when you need another."

We soon made our way to the living room to join Dona and Beth. As soon as we walked in the room, Beth said, "You didn't tell me they just had a grandson!"

ARGH! I totally forgot Barry and Dona were expecting a grandbaby. "Barry, I totally forgot! It's a boy?"

Dona jumped in, "He sure is! All four of them are boys!" She pulled out her phone and showed me a picture, telling me his name was Michael Andrew Kene. She then showed pictures of the other three grandsons too.

We spent the next hour or so getting to know each other. I was surprised to learn that Barry didn't play golf, but he enjoyed relaxing by playing a game on his phone. It also surprised me to learn that he had not always had a career in consulting but had started out as a laborer! Dona was interesting too. She had homeschooled their kids before homeschooling was really accepted, and she made custom ceramic dolls as a hobby!

Though everyone seemed to be enjoying the conversation, Beth eventually cut her eyes in my direction, letting me know she thought we had stayed long enough. We politely ended the conversation and our visit, all of us agreeing we should do this again. Soon Beth and I were on our way home.

In the car, Beth said, "I really enjoyed visiting with Barry and Dona. They are nice people. Dona and I really got along well. The dolls she makes are beautiful!"

I looked at Beth with an affirming smile and replied, "I told you I want to be like Barry when I grow up."

"And I told you to stop it!" Beth exclaimed as she playfully slapped me on the shoulder.

On the way home we discussed what it was that made Barry and Dona so different.

That night I bought my first tool in the Bible study software. Even so, I looked forward even more to Barry's commentary on the new words more than my new study tool notes.

RETHINKING HONOR

Tuesday soon rolled around, and I eagerly left the house looking forward to the coffee and study time with Barry. I found him waiting for me at the door when I arrived. In a minute we had ordered our coffee and made our way to the usual seats. Barry opened, as always, with a short prayer, then he asked me, "Tell me what you've learned so far about love."

I didn't quite expect that question right up front. "Well, I've learned that I have a lot more to learn."

Barry laughed. "Me too. Let me caution you though, learning about love isn't an academic exercise, and it's not like a new skill you've learned for work. What I mean is that you can't just figure this out and put it into place. It's a God thing, and it requires a heart change."

I paused a moment as I realized I was trying to force this, but I didn't know how to make my heart change. "Barry," I replied, "I don't know where to start. I am so far off from where I need to be, and I feel like it would be easier if I could just start over."

"We can't change the past," Barry leaned forward, "I look at it as part of what makes us unique, kind of like the spices in a recipe. As you grow more, you adjust those spices so the result tastes good. Remember though, you must start, and I've found the best way to do that is to ask God to open your eyes to opportunities to show His love and to make you aware of things you need to change. I also ask Him to help me *act* on what He shows me."

This all made sense to me. I knew I needed to change, and with a glimmer of hope I realized God could help me with this.

Barry then said, "Speaking of that, let's get to the next attributes of love. We'll try to do three today, starting in verse 5 where we're told 'love does not behave dishonorably, it is not selfish, and it does not become angry.'

"The first of the three pertains to dishonorable behavior. Some versions use the word rude," Barry continued. "I find a nuance here that we don't necessarily see in the other words."

He went on to explain, "The word rude has a cultural context. For example, in the United States it is rude to be late. In other countries, this is not only acceptable, but expected. That's why I like 'dishonorable behavior' better. You could also say inappropriate behavior or indecency."

I interjected, "When I read love 'does not behave dishonorably,' it made me think of the importance of honor in Asian culture. I learned a lot about this from a high school friend. His name was Míng Jié. He and his family had emigrated from China. He was always careful not to act in a way that would dishonor his family."

"That's a good way of thinking of it," replied Barry. He was quiet for a moment, and I could tell he was thinking. "I've never thought of it this way before, but you could say that our behavior shouldn't dishonor our God."

I rubbed my chin for a moment as I looked at the ceiling. This made me think about honoring your parents in a different light. I finally broke the silence with, "Yeah, I like that. That makes sense to me."

Barry opened his notebook and made a note. I followed his lead and did the same.

After we both finished writing, Barry continued, "Likewise, you could also think of disgracing someone else. For example, have you ever seen someone talk down to their spouse in front of others? Or what about their children? The reverse is true too. Have you seen children behave in a dishonorable fashion toward their parents?"

I nodded in agreement, realizing how often I saw this exact behavior, even in myself and my own children. I then replied, "My mom always says that children don't respect their parents anymore."

Barry said, "I'm probably close to your mom's age, and we certainly grew up in a different world, but we weren't perfect either. The next phrase is also one your mom might comment on: 'love is not selfish.' This reminds me of First Corinthians 10:24 where it says, 'Let no one seek his own good but the good of the other.'"

With excitement I interjected, "I noticed a few places in the Bible that refer to 'selfish ambition,' and one of them is right before the listing of the Fruit of the Spirit in Galatians 5!"

Barry exclaimed, "Ah! Good find! That's part of the 'deeds of the flesh,' which are the sinful contrast to the Fruit of the Spirit."

Going deeper into these words made me realize how much I needed to change.

"It seems like many of these words are about putting others first and treating them well." As I said this, I realized how little love I showed others, even my own wife.

Barry said, "I think that's why the Golden Rule is so important. It helps us to frame this right. We should treat others like we want to be treated! This is one of the most famous moral codes ever, and it came right from Jesus' mouth. How often do you think about your actions that way though?"

"Never?" I replied.

"That's not uncommon, Chuck. We live in a very self-centered world where it's all about us – it's all about me."

Barry took another sip of his coffee, then continued "The last phrase today has the word 'anger' in it, but this is a difficult word to translate. The Greek word translated as anger here is only used a couple of times in the Bible; believe it or not, it's not the same word used for anger in most other places in the New Testament. The literal translation is, 'love is not provoked,' and though it can refer to positive or negative emotions, I think the context here points to the negative."

He then opened his notebook and read, "This Greek word is also the root word for paroxysm. I didn't know what that meant when I first read it, do you?"

I shook my head as I replied, "No, I don't."

Barry said, "It's a sudden outburst of anger. And the opposite of this word in Greek means to deflect or avoid. All of this leads me to believe this isn't just being angry, it is about how you respond when someone attempts to torque you or incite you."

Confused, I replied, "But that makes it seem like we are to just take abuse!"

"That could be an interesting study too," Barry said. After finishing his coffee, he continued, "Let me offer an alternative way of seeing it. Sometimes others attempt to get us riled up, either to have a scuffle with us – or as often happens – to stir up our anger toward another person. We can often diffuse the situation by not letting them get to us. In these two cases, someone walking in love would just take the high road."

Barry reached over to take my empty cup, but I interrupted, "Barry, can we pray together? Today's study has been very personal for me. I'm guilty of all of this."

Barry said, "Sure, let's do that now." He leaned across the table, placing his hand on my shoulder as he prayed for me. Then, as he pulled his hand away, he said, "Chuck, you aren't alone. We are all inclined to live by the flesh, and unlike the way it works in the rest of the world, you cannot fix yourself. Even if you started showing these traits to others in your life, the love we are talking about only comes from God. That's why these attributes are called the Fruit of the Spirit. They come from Him. Our study is opening your eyes to something better, but you have to let go and let God begin to change you."

Barry stood up and picked up our coffee cups as he looked me in the eyes and said, "And I know you're going to do that. I believe your heart is ready."

BABY STEPS

After getting to the office, I had trouble paying attention to my work. I kept thinking about our talk and remembering how poorly I had treated others, so I decided to do something about it. I went to the breakroom and made two cups of coffee. I then took one to Marshall and said, "I'm really pleased with your work on the deal we won on Friday."

He took the coffee from my extended hand with a puzzled look, simply replying, "Thanks."

As I walked back to my office, I mulled over how he didn't even know how to respond to a compliment from me. I closed my door and sat down, putting my head in my hands as I prayed to God again that He would help me to be more loving. When I finished praying, I texted Beth and told her I'd like to take her out for dinner tonight.

She replied, "Is everything okay?"

I answered, "Find a babysitter. All is well. I love you."

When I arrived home, I was happy to see Dana, our neighbor's daughter, was already at our house to watch the kids. I gave each of the kids and hug and a kiss, then walked out to the garage with Beth. As we got in my car, I asked, "Where do you want to go to eat? It's your choice."

"Honestly, Long John Silvers. I'm craving their chicken strips!" Beth replied.

Beth knew I preferred a proper restaurant, but I bit my tongue and we headed to Long John Silvers.

Over chicken, fish, and hush puppies, I told Beth of the conversations Barry and I had been having about love. I then said, "I'm really sorry Beth, I've not been a very loving husband."

Beth tried to comfort me, "I know you love me, and you love the kids too, but I also know you work in a very stressful job."

While that was all true, I knew I wasn't loving her very well, especially in the way I showed her love, and I had decided to change that from now on.

Over the next week, I eagerly dug into the rest of the passage in 1 Corinthians 13. The next attributes of love also stood out to me: "it does not keep a record of wrongs, it does not rejoice at unrighteousness, but rejoices with the truth." Thrilled to find that I might at least have two things right. I am honest with people, I think, and I don't rejoice at unrighteousness. But I sure kept a record of wrongs.

Two incidents stood out to me – times when I let this bad habit get in the way of friendships. The first was a high school friend named Amanda. I really liked Amanda, but I'm not sure the feeling was mutual. She always asked for car rides, promising to pay me gas money later. I started noticing she never paid though, so I began tracking. After 40 rides without payment, I had enough, and I never gave her another ride.

The second was similar but happened in college. I started noticing Bruce was always happy when I came to hang out with him, but he never came to hang out with me, so I started tracking it. Sure enough, I was right. After 20 visits with no reciprocation, I quit hanging out with Bruce.

The thing was, I really liked Amanda and Bruce. In fact, Bruce was one of my closest friends, but it was more than I could handle to feel like I was being wronged.

On Friday the team did a great job getting a proposal ready for a good prospect before we left for the weekend, so I offered to take them all out for pizza after work. I was disappointed when a few people didn't join us though, especially Roxie, who never seemed to join our events. It seemed as if she didn't appreciate my offer. But Marshall, Susie, and two other analysts joined us, as well as Deb and our technical liaison Chris.

Saturday, I offered to let Beth go shopping with her sister, and I took the kids to the park. It was a beautiful day with low humidity, but the sun freely gave of its warmth. The kids took advantage of this by playing in the spray pad for the last time of the year. They would soon shut it off after the Labor Day weekend.

After Beth came home that evening, she gave me a big hug and said, "Thank you, handsome. That was a real treat. I love you!"

It was at that moment that I realized that before today I couldn't think of a single time I had offered to watch the kids on a Saturday without being asked.

MORE TO THE STORY

On Sunday at church, a group of young adults shared their plans for a mission trip over the holiday break. They were going to Ecuador to help build a house and work in an orphanage. They took up a special offering, and their enthusiasm made me want to help. I was proud to give them 50 dollars.

When Tuesday rolled around, I arrived at the coffee shop a few minutes early. The aroma reminded me of my grandma's house when she baked pies. As I paid for my coffee and Barry's too, Annie asked, "Did you have a good Labor Day Weekend?"

"I sure did. How about you, Annie?" I asked.

"It was good. I worked on Saturday, but we're always closed on Sunday, and I had Monday off too."

She then asked, "Would you like a fresh girdle scone?"

"What's a girdle scone?" I replied.

"Girdle scones are Scottish, but we use a bit more sugar. They're baked on the griddle instead of in the oven. I think 'girdle' is how the Scottish say 'griddle.' Let me get one for you."

Annie grabbed a small plate and took a triangular scone fresh off the griddle.

She then asked me, "Do you go to church with Mr. Kene?"

"I do."

"He's a really kind man." She replied.

"Oh? What makes you say that?"

Annie seemed hesitant, but she wanted to say more. After a moment she continued, "It's kind of a long story. I got pregnant in high school, and I barely graduated before giving birth to Garrett. His dad didn't want anything to do with us, and he didn't even have a job anyhow."

She added, "I started working as a waitress in a restaurant where I met Mr. Kene. After learning a bit of my story, he asked if I would meet him here to talk about my future."

Annie had a tear in her eye as she continued, "I agreed. He told me he noticed how hard I worked and how I wanted the best for my son. He then did the most amazing thing. He offered to pay for two classes a semester at the community college so I could get a degree."

I didn't know how to respond to this. "I had no idea. That was really kind. What are you studying?"

"Right now, just the basics, but I'm going to get a degree in business administration. He also helped me get a job here. The owners are good people. Everyone that works here has had something happen that derailed their plans for life. Most of us are taking classes of some sort. They pay us well for what we do, and when it's slow they let us study."

I was dumbfounded. There's no way this place could be profitable with a plan like that, but they sure seemed to be doing well. And Annie, she seemed so happy. I was puzzled by it all, thinking how tough her life must be right now.

I then noticed a tip jar by the register. Barry always put a $5 bill in it. Today I did the same. "Thank you for sharing, Annie."

Just then, Barry walked in, and I told him, "I got your coffee today, Barry."

Annie piped up, "And here's a fresh girdle scone too!"

Barry rolled his eyes at Annie and said, "You know I'm trying to watch what I eat, and you know I love your scones!"

Annie's smile went from ear-to-ear as she said to Barry, "You haven't had one in a while, and I made these just for you!"

"Vanilla blueberry?" Barry asked.

"Yep!" Annie replied as she handed Barry his scone on a small plate.

After sitting down, Barry prayed, then asked, "How's your week been?"

He took a bite of his scone, and I did too. Before I could reply to his question he said, "These things are evil, Annie! You know I can't resist them when they're fresh!"

Barry was so right. The rich and buttery scones had a touch of sweetness, and just the right amount of vanilla and blueberries. I gave Annie a thumbs up as I said, "I've never had one before. They are really good!" I thought I saw Annie smiling again out of the corner of my eye.

I then said, "Barry, I feel like my eyes have been opened. I'm trying to find opportunities to show love to others."

Neither of us talked as we both enjoyed another bite or two of our scones.

Barry reminded me, "Don't forget, you cannot do this on your own. If you aren't asking God to help you identify those areas and fill your heart with love, you're still trying to fix yourself."

I realized the truth of Barry's words. I opened my notebook, and jotted down, "Ask God to help you love more, and then listen! Do what He leads you to do."

Barry waited for me to finish writing, then he said, "Let's get into our study!"

"The next word we're looking at is often translated 'resentful,' but I don't think that captures the meaning well. The version we've been reading says love, 'does not keep a record of wrongs.' I think that hits the nail on the head. I'm embarrassed to admit this, but I've told people in the past that if they hurt me, I would hurt them back."

I interrupted, "Yes! This one hit me hard when I first read it." I then wondered if I sounded excited about this. Calming down, I continued, "I've often said something similar, 'Burn me once, shame on you. Burn me twice, shame on me.'"

"It looks like we have something in common," Barry replied. "Unfortunately, it's nothing to be proud of."

I debated telling him about Amanda and Bruce but was afraid of what he would think.

He continued, "I think God is our example for each of these attributes, and this one stands out most to me. Imagine if God were keeping score of our sins. Instead, He allowed our sins to be totally wiped clean. We shouldn't keep score of sins others commit against us either."

Barry finished off his scone, then continued, "I think the version we're studying gets the next one right too: 'love does not rejoice at unrighteousness but rejoices with the truth.'"

He then looked at me as he said, "Not rejoicing at unrighteousness might seem self-explanatory, but I think it's worth digging into. What does unrighteousness even mean? Any ideas?"

I stammered, "Well, I don't know. I guess not righteous. I know that's not what you're looking for though. I hadn't really thought about it. Maybe not living right."

"You're actually pretty close," Barry replied. "But let's dig deeper. The lexicons say this word is referring to going against standards of right or acceptable conduct. But what is that? We must remember that Paul was a Jew and thought about things through a Jewish lens. Right conduct for Paul would likely have meant following God's Law or the Law of Christ. Though this isn't defined, it's reasonable to think it's referring to the two greatest commandments: loving God with everything we have and loving our neighbors as we love ourselves. This sits well with my spirit since these two commandments summarize the Ten Commandments."

Barry took a long sip of coffee, then he continued, "All that said, we could simplify this, I think. Love leads to righteousness, and the lack of it leads to unrighteousness, which is sinful living. I think Paul is simply saying that love does not rejoice at sinful living."

Barry finished his coffee, setting the cup down, then saying, "But now we have what appears to be a contrasting statement that identifies what love does rejoice in: the truth. When I first read this, I thought to myself that the opposite of unrighteousness is not truth but righteousness. But then I read Ephesians 4:24, where Paul states we are to put on the new man 'in righteousness and holiness that comes from truth.' So, truth produces righteousness and holiness. But we still haven't defined what truth is. Is it just being honest, or is there more to it?"

"Truth sounds like honesty to me," I replied.

"Honesty's important, and I think it applies, but there's another layer. Let's keep digging. In John 14:6 Jesus tells us that He is the truth. Reasoning through that: righteousness and holiness come from the truth, and the truth is Jesus. We should rejoice in Jesus, the truth, from whom comes our righteousness and holiness."

I inhaled slowly, then as I exhaled, I replied, "That's deep."

"It is," Barry replied, "and that's a good place to end today. Next week we'll start studying the last five attributes, which I think are the hardest to describe. Be sure you read up on them ahead of time."

I stood and picked up our coffee cups, and as we walked out, Barry said, "We covered a lot today. I want to encourage you to study this more for yourself; don't just take my word for any of this. Remember, I'm just a student too, and you may find things in your studies that I miss."

I guess I thought Barry knew all the answers. It was only then I realized that just last week Barry made a note of something *I* had said! After that realization, I replied, "Thanks for that, Barry. I needed that reminder."

"No one has it all figured out. We're all learning and growing." Barry winked at me and waved as he walked off, "I'll see you next Tuesday, Chuck."

THE INTERRUPTION

Late Tuesday afternoon I met with the team to brainstorm creative ways to retain Sunshine Healthcare, one of our principal clients who had been with us for years. We had a service misstep with them this year and also found ourselves being undercut in price by a new competitor. Just as we dialed into a creative zone, Sandy knocked lightly and then opened the door to the conference room.

She looked at me and quietly said, "Chuck, we need to talk."

This made me furious. She knew not to interrupt us during a brainstorming session! We can so easily lose the creative flow. Trying to hide my emotions, I curtly replied, "Not now, Sandy."

"Chuck, we *really* need to talk," she said seriously.

Having little patience for interruptions like this, I replied, "Did you not hear me? Not now! I'll get to you when we're done."

Sandy turned around and walked out, slamming the door behind her.

The room was silent, the interruption having the expected effect. I was livid, and I'm sure my face showed it. The Red Giant was dying to make an appearance, but I held it together. I then focused on refreshing everyone for the process at hand. It took a moment, but the team soon got back in their groove. After a solid 45 minutes of great brainstorming, I left the team to work out the details. I felt confident we had put together a strategy to retain Sunshine Healthcare.

I headed straight to Sandy's office to find out what was so important that she felt she could interrupt us. Just as I was about to say something, Sandy blurted out, "I was trying to tell you that Score! was calling for you, and they said it was urgent."

Score! Security, or Score! as we referred to them, was our preferred vendor for network security testing. They employed Brazilian hackers who were known as the best network penetration testers in the business. As I turned to leave the room, Sandy said, "It's bad, Chuck. They had an employee arrested for hacking. It was Leandro."

I closed my eyes and whispered to myself, "Please no!" Leandro was the best they had, and on our most important accounts. I then turned to Sandy and asked, "What else do you know?"

"They are issuing a press release soon. I've started drafting a communication to our customers that you'll need to review. You need to call Tim at Score! now."

I headed straight to my office and shut the door. After talking with Tim, I realized this was worse than I thought. Leandro had been found with data belonging to some of their clients. Tim reassured me that no data from our clients had been found, but I knew Leandro was on the team performing network security testing for Sunshine. I guess it was good that they proactively notified us, but this was a publicity nightmare, and Tim was not going to delay the press release much longer.

As soon as I hung up the phone, I messaged Sandy, "Clear my calendar and bring in the communication piece you're working on."

For the next 20 minutes, Sandy and I brainstormed two messages to our clients, the most important being for those using Score! and the second message for all other clients. And then I had to call Tracy, the Chief Technology Officer at Sunshine. The timing could not have been worse. Tracy expected an updated proposal from me, instead I showed up delivering a strong reason for him to use another vendor.

"I'm sorry to hear that Chuck," Tracy replied. "I'll report this to our security committee right away. I expect updates daily, and I expect Southside to perform a full investigation."

I replied with assurance, "Of course, Tracy. We're your partner in this."

After I hung up the phone, I buried my head in my hands. In vain had we just spent the last hour working on this strategy. I stared at my computer screen, then noticed it was September 11. It should have been a solemn day, but no one even mentioned it. And now we just received news of our own disaster, of sorts. I finally collected my thoughts and headed back to the conference room to tell the team.

I called Beth at 5:30 that afternoon to tell her I would be really late. She asked, "What's going on? You don't sound like yourself."

"Honey, this is really bad," I replied. "An employee at one of our vendors went rogue and started stealing data. I won't bore you with the details, but the important part is that some of our clients could have a data breach as a result. This could hurt business bad, and our income too."

"I'll pray," Beth replied. "I love you."

"I love you too. I've got to go." I hung up my phone to focus on work.

The days blurred together for the rest of the week. During the day I spent hours on the phone with clients doing damage-control. Then our team would meet in the evenings to understand the extent of the damage and what we needed to do to retain the most at-risk clients.

This made it very hard to think about love or even read the Bible amidst the crisis. Even so, I made myself keep up with my reading plan each night. For the first time in my life, I found solace and comfort in morning prayer.

Southside had always been a high-pressure environment, but the office tension now hovered in the red zone. Large bonuses for everyone hinged on our retaining clients and gaining business. We now faced a seemingly insurmountable challenge.

During our Thursday night meeting, Walter lashed out at me, "Have you lost your edge? Most of our customers don't even know about this, but you insist on telling them! What happened to 'what they don't know won't hurt them?'"

With all eyes on me, I sternly replied, "What's wrong with doing the right thing? Frankly, I want to be able to sleep at night!"

Walter stood up, pointed his finger at me, then yelled, "I think your new-found religion is killing our profit! Do you think Beth will be able to sleep at night when you don't get that fat bonus check?" He then stuck his middle fingers in the air as he stormed out of the room. No one said a word for at least 15 minutes as they pretended to work.

Breaking the uneasy silence, I asked, "Deb, could you pull up the spreadsheet once more? Who else do we need to contact?" Once we pinpointed the remaining five customers who would be impacted by our outsourcing with Score!, I sent everyone home.

SEEING THE BEST
IN OTHERS

After working another long day on Friday and most of the day on Saturday, I didn't feel like going to church on Sunday. By the time Tuesday
came around, I didn't really have the time for coffee, but I didn't want to
let Barry down. I hurried in a few minutes late to find Barry already seated
when I arrived.

He was the only one in the coffee shop, unusual for a Tuesday. As soon
as I walked through the door I said, "I am so sorry I'm late Barry!" I quickly
walked over and shook his hand.

Barry replied, "Are you okay, Chuck? You look a bit haggard."

"Is it that noticeable?" I replied.

"Well, your eyes look tired, and you seem more rushed than I've seen
you before." Barry then pointed to my shoes. I looked down and saw I was
wearing two different shoes!

"I can't believe I did that! I was running late when I left, and I guess I was
in too much of a hurry."

"Well, at least the shoes are the same color!" Barry replied.

I tried to smile, but it was forced.

Barry then asked, "Before we pray, Chuck, why don't you tell me what's going on in your life? It's obvious something is wrong."

"It's been really bad at work," I replied. "One of our vendors had a major cyber event that affects many of our customers, and now we have some key deals on the line. There is no good way to tell this story to our clients, and the entire team is stretched thin due to the long hours and the stress. I've been praying about my days and trying to keep love in my mind, but I've blown it more than once. And then Walter, the guy we've met here a couple of times, accused me of losing my edge. We had it out in front of the team."

Barry seemed to be thinking, and he didn't say anything for what seemed to be minutes as he sipped his coffee. Finally, he said, "You're going through a lot right now. I don't know if these are tests or trials, but I can tell it's really stretching you. How about we say a prayer and then postpone our study until next week?"

"I would appreciate the prayer," I replied, "but I don't want to postpone. Just being here today reminds me of how much I need this."

Barry nodded his head ever so slightly. "That sounds like wisdom speaking. Let's pray."

He began, "Father, grant us Your presence today and open our hearts and minds to be fully aware of You and Your goodness. Protect us as we traverse the day and enable us to be good reflections of Jesus. Help us to keep You, Your love, and our love for others in the forefront of our minds. Amen."

Barry leaned forward in his seat, resting his elbows on his knees and clasping his hands together. "Chuck, we're pivoting into a difficult part of this passage, and I think it's important to think about the context as we learn about it. Paul is writing to the church about church relations. While love is not just for believers to exhibit toward other believers, these last four phrases may be easier to grasp with this audience in mind. When we are thinking of other believers, do we see and assume the best in them, or do we see and assume the worst in them?"

I was dumbfounded, and my reply showed it. "I had never thought about considering the audience when reading the Bible! I guess I just thought it was written to me."

With his comforting smile, Barry said, "It is written *for* you and for all believers, but maybe not *to* you. You see, by understanding the original audience – who Paul was writing *to* – passages sometimes come across differently, with new insights."

Still absorbing this, I slowly replied, "That makes sense."

"Today we'll start with 'love bears all things,'" Barry continued. "The Greek word for 'bears' is stegō, and like we've seen with other words already, a simple translation doesn't really do it justice."

After pausing to take a sip of his coffee, Barry continued, "When I first read that love bears all things, my mind substituted the word 'tolerates' for 'bears,' and while that is a possible translation, it sounds very close to 'love endures all things,' which we'll come to later. For that reason, I don't think that's what this is saying."

Barry picked up his journal and pointed to the leather cover as he said, "This word can also mean to cover or protect, like this leather cover protects the paper inside or like a raincoat protects the wearer. Or it can mean to hold back, like a tight ship holds back water. With that in mind, let me read what I found in my studies."

After putting on his glasses, Barry opened his journal and thumbed through a few pages before saying, "Here it is! 'Love covers all things,' in the sense of 'covering with a cloak of love.'[1] You could also say it's a 'love that throws a cloak of silence over what is displeasing in another person.'"[2]

"I don't think I understand. Can you say it a different way?" I asked.

Looking at me over the top of his glasses, Barry smirked, "I told you this was difficult."

Barry continued, "When I was studying this, I noticed how similar this is to Proverbs 10:12, 'Hatred stirs up strife, but love covers over all offenses' and 1 Peter 4:8 'love covers a large number of sins.' This leads me to believe Paul is referring to our ability to look past the sins of another and using the

---

[1] Bromiley, Geoffrey W., Gerhard Kittel, and Gerhard Friedrich. 1985. *Theological Dictionary of the New Testament*. Eerdmans.

[2] Walter Bauer; Frederick William Danker. 2000. *A Greek-English Lexicon of the New Testament and Other Early Christian Literature, 3rd ed.* (BDAG) University of Chicago Press.

noted contrast in Proverbs 10:12 to not allow dissension to be stirred up. You should probably write those verses down."

I opened my journal and noted the verses.

Barry continued, "I would be remiss if I didn't mention how this reflects God too. According to Romans 4:7, Jesus' sacrifice covered our sins."

I jotted that verse down too. "Barry, I'm still trying to understand. I think you're saying we should not talk about the problems in someone else's life."

"You are very close, Chuck, but can you carry that one step further?" Barry took a sip of his coffee as he waited for me to reply.

I pondered what I just said for a moment. "I think so. We should also protect people when we hear others talking about them when they're not present."

"That's it, Chuck! One other thing, it's rarely productive to share the rumors being spread about a person with them, as it often just upsets them."

I thought about how I shared rumors with people thinking it would help them. I wondered how much harm that had caused.

Barry continued, "Next we have, 'Love believes all things.' I think this is the most difficult attribute of love. Some believe this is referring to fully having faith in the things of God, and the phrase could be used in that way, but the context doesn't seem right. Instead, this seems to be saying that we should be trusting of people, not treating their words with cynicism or distrust. Love sees the best in people and expects them to be honorable. This is especially true within the family of believers, as we should expect the best from other believers, that they are honorable and trustworthy people."

I thought about how I rarely believed most anyone – skeptical or even cynical of most people. One thing sales has taught me is that people are going to tell you what benefits them most. I began learning this lesson long ago though. My own dad, who preached the importance of honesty, lied to get out of a speeding ticket. After that, I always wondered what else he lied about.

As if he could read my mind, Barry asked, "Here's a tough question for you: do you struggle to trust people in the church?"

Holding back a little, I replied, "Sometimes. Sometimes I feel like Christians take advantage of other Christians."

"They do," Barry said. "And there's a lesson for us in this. No one should ever have reason to question our integrity, especially brothers and sisters in the Lord. Ephesians 4:25 says we should speak truth to our neighbor, 'for we are members of one another.'"

"Barry, we know that's not always true. Good people lie all the time!" I replied.

"You're right," Barry said. "Even so, we should give other believers the benefit of the doubt. To your point though, sometimes we find someone in the church who professes to be a Christian and deliberately sins, and that includes being deceptive. The Bible tells us in Luke 17:3 that we should rebuke a brother who sins and forgive them if they repent."

I found myself fidgeting a bit as I replied, "I feel like I'm going to struggle with this one."

"None of this is easy, and I think most of it makes us feel vulnerable. But believers should be the first to exhibit love, and that includes trusting and being trustworthy."

Barry took the last drink of his coffee, then just as he got ready to talk, he paused to think before saying, "Telling it like it is, I found this one hard too. I had to spend time studying and praying on this one."

As Barry began to stand, he said, "We'll wrap up here today."

I stood at the same time and took our coffee mugs to the tray.

LOSING IT

On the drive to the office, I thought of how glad I was to have made time for coffee with Barry. Our time together stretched my mind, but I also felt recharged.

It didn't take long for the direction of my day to shift, however. I walked into the office and the bad news hit almost immediately. Apparently, Markson Strategic Enterprises, a supplier of military equipment, chose a key competitor over us. To make matters worse, this was the second potential client we had lost to them recently. Everyone in the office was uptight.

I went to my office to see what else awaited me. While reading through my messages, I heard a knock at my door. It was Mr. Barton. Usually, I had meetings with him in his office, not mine.

Startled, I said, "Yes, sir. What can I do for you?"

He came into the office and shut the door, but he didn't bother sitting. "I'm sure you've heard we lost the Markson contract." He stood at the door with his arms crossed. "This is a big deal, Chuck. I'm beginning to think we've lost our edge."

I felt my face flushing. He sounded like Walter.

He continued, "We haven't won either of the last two big deals, and we've lost two important customers this year, and I hear we may lose another. I'm told your head is not in the game like it once was."

He stared at me for a moment. Just as I was about to say something, he said, "Just remember, your bonus and your future depend on this. I hope I can count on you." Mr. Barton opened the door and walked out before I could reply.

For the rest of the week, I arrived early each day, and we had late-night working sessions over pizza at the office. By the time Saturday rolled around, I knew I wouldn't have much of a weekend either. We had planned to take the kids to the zoo, but I couldn't get away. I also missed church again on Sunday.

When I arrived at the office on Monday, all hopes of an easier week were dashed when I read the post-mortem on the Markson deal. Two of our mid-tier analysts didn't get through their analysis fast enough, and we found mistakes in what they provided. Mr. Barton soon emailed me, "Fire these two analysts who messed up. They aren't performing, and everyone needs to know how serious this is."

I felt sick to my stomach. These two had not performed well, but we usually wouldn't fire someone over this. I knew there was no point in arguing, so I called them into my office and let them go.

The stress was palpable. Everyone wondered who else might be terminated. The only good news of the day came as a glimmer of hope that we might retain Sunshine Healthcare. Mr. Barton sent me an email with the details accompanied by his message, "You know what to do. CLOSE THIS DEAL."

I pulled together a small team of mid-tier analysts and a few other support people, and we began to review the notes. I suspected Walter might have some insight that could help, as he had dealt with something similar. I sent him a message, "Can you give us some thoughts on the Sunshine retention effort? We need all the help we can get."

"Sorry, Chuck," he replied. "I'm tied up on a big deal of my own with a potential new customer. You can handle it. You're a big boy."

I could feel my face turn red and slammed my hand against the conference room table in anger as I yelled, "What. Is. His. Problem!" Pretending nothing had happened, no one looked up from their screens.

I had seen this before and knew *exactly* what was going on. Walter didn't want to help us with this deal because he wouldn't benefit from it. But the company couldn't afford to lose Sunshine, especially right now, and this left my team at a real disadvantage.

I stormed out of the room and went to the breakroom. In a moment of stress, I devoured two bags of peanuts. I then realized I had to regain my composure. I took a few deep breaths and said a short prayer as I walked back to the conference room.

I did my best to motivate the team. We were down two analysts, and I needed the team to be resourceful and get the data we needed. It would mean more late nights.

Tuesday morning, I found it hard to prioritize having coffee with Barry with everything going on at work. I finally justified it by answering a few emails before leaving home.

When I opened the garage, I noticed the coolness of the morning. It was officially fall now, and the cool weather would soon be here to stay a while. On the way to the coffee shop, I wondered when the leaves would start to change colors. Beth and I loved to take Sunday drives when the autumn leaves were at their peak. I wondered if we'd get that privilege this year.

Barry stood up to greet me as I walked in late again. Shaking my hand, he said, "How are you making it, Chuck? I noticed you weren't at church again this week, and I'm worried about you."

Annie brought my coffee over as I sat down. "Good morning, Chuck. Here's your coffee!"

I carefully took a sip of the hot coffee, then I recounted the last week to Barry. He listened attentively. When I finished, I took another small drink and looked toward the windows.

Barry remained quiet until I turned back toward him. He then said, "Be careful that you don't let your job become your god."

"That won't happen," I replied.

"Good," said Barry. "Let's get started so you can get to work. I'm hoping we can get through the rest of the love attributes in First Corinthians 13 today."

After praying, Barry asked, "Did you happen to read ahead any this week?" When I replied that I hadn't, he said, "Well, this may be just for you today."

I wondered what he meant by that.

Barry continued, "Our first phrase is 'love hopes all things.' I used to believe this was saying that the believer who operates in love should hope for the best in others. I know that doesn't make sense after what we learned about believing all things, but I reasoned that belief was more about all the stuff happening today – in the present – and that hope was about the future. As I studied this more though, I came to believe this refers more to a driving force within us, not our thoughts about others."

"Can you say that differently?" I asked. "I don't understand what you're saying."

"Sure," Barry replied. "Our *hope* is about our relationship with God, not our opinions about others. Remember how I said Paul would have been driven by Semitic culture, specifically Jewish culture?"

I replied, "Yeah?"

Barry continued, "Well, that context will help us understand this better."

Barry took a sip of his coffee, then opened his journal to a bookmarked page. "In the ancient Jewish culture, hope did not mean wishful thinking; hope meant to trust in God. The Jews trusted that God would protect and help them."

Looking down at his journal, he continued, "We could go to many places in the Bible for an example, but I like Psalms 56 where David writes, 'in God I trust; I am not afraid.' The New Testament teaches this same truth also. The verse – I'm sure you've heard before – is Romans 8:28. That verse tells us that all things work together for good for those who love God and are called according to His purpose."

I quickly opened my notebook and wrote down Psalm 56 and Romans 8.

"Pay close attention, the real point is this," Barry continued. "Love recognizes that the 'world' is not in control. God is in control. When we know that God is in control, we can confidently act in love, even when doing so might seem like it's against our best interests. Love looks to the future with optimistic trust – knowing that all things work together for our good because we love God and are called according to His purpose."

I couldn't hide my emotions. I wiped a tear from my eye, hoping Barry had not noticed. Deep down I realized how deeply I trusted in myself and my abilities, not God. Sure, I believed God loved and cared for me, but was He going to close this deal for us?

Just then, Barry removed his glasses and interjected, "Be careful with this one, Chuck. Many people believe that 'all things work together for good for those who love God' means that nothing bad will ever happen to them. Some also like to think of God like a genie in a bottle, as if He will provide for all their desires. It's important to remember that we can have the confidence that all things will work together for our good, but that doesn't mean all things are going to go according to our plans."

As I made a few notes on what Barry had just said, he put his glasses back on, opened his notebook, and thumbed through the pages.

"Next, we move on to 'Love endures all things.'" He then read from his journal again, "The Greek word for 'endures' means 'to maintain a belief or course of action in the face of opposition, stand one's ground, hold out, endure.'[3] It would be easy here to say this refers to how we should continue in adversity, especially when persecuted for our beliefs. While I believe that's true, in the context of these verses describing love, this probably refers to our actions or activities toward others. If we serve others and they act ungrateful or our work feels unappreciated, we should continue to persevere in doing good."

"So, we should love others whether they appreciate it or not?" I asked.

"That's it – a lot simpler than the last one." Barry then stood up and picked up our coffee mugs.

Curiously, I asked, "I thought we had one more today?"

Barry replied, "We do. We'll cover it on the way out."

---

[3] Walter Bauer; Frederick William Danker. 2000. *A Greek-English Lexicon of the New Testament and Other Early Christian Literature, 3rd ed.* (BDAG) University of Chicago Press.

As we walked out together, Barry said, "We've come to the end of this passage, and we've covered a lot about what biblical love is, but we're not quite done studying this yet, we'll meet again next week. The final piece we'll cover today is 'love never ends.'

"I think Paul is saying that godly love stays present at all times. Long after many other things have ceased to exist, love will still be there."

Barry stopped and turned toward me. He laid his hand on my shoulder and said a prayer for me as we went our separate ways. I took a deep breath realizing the rest of my day might not be as refreshing as this moment.

LOST IT

Our teams kept busy crunching the numbers all of Tuesday and Wednesday to evaluate the best way we could present our services to Sunshine. Knowing the importance of this deal, in particular, set everyone on edge, but by Thursday morning, our work seemed to be paying off. It looked as though Sunshine might renew!

When Walter heard the update at Thursday morning's meeting, he suddenly became much more cooperative. He looked at Mr. Barton and said, "I might have some information that could help close this deal."

Enthusiastically, Mr. Barton replied, "That's the team spirit, Walter! Jump in and help where you can on this crucial deal!"

My blood began to boil! What a mercenary hack! Here's Walter, coming in at the last minute and positioning himself as the savior – the whole reason we retain Sunshine. I couldn't diss him though. I needed the information he had to increase our chances. Even so, I had worked hard on this, and now he would get the credit for closing this deal.

The team convened in the conference room, pushing hard to get a workable proposal to Sunshine. As much as I hated to admit it, Walter supplied us with a treasure trove of great suggestions, plus he also stepped in to help with a few sticking points. However, I let it get under my skin when the team looked to *him* for advice on how to proceed. *Don't they know who's in charge of this deal?*

My frustration was eating at me but by late Thursday afternoon the odds of renewing Sunshine had greatly improved, and I could see the mood around the office lifting. I emailed Tracy with the proposal at 5:00 and then sent the team home. This was the first time we had left this early in weeks.

I thought I would surprise Beth and not let her know I'd be leaving on time for a change. When I walked into the house, David was the first to spot me. "Daddy! Daddy's home!"

Beth suddenly appeared and exclaimed, "You're home! I'm so happy to see you. Come join us! We're just sitting down for supper."

I grabbed a plate from the cabinet, sat at the table, and then shocked everyone by saying, "Let's say a prayer before we eat."

For the first time in as long as I could remember we had a nice time together as a family while eating supper. The kids were so well-behaved, and I even thought of asking Beth about her day before she asked me about mine.

After supper, I quickly texted Barry to let him know we might close the deal that had caused me so much stress for weeks.

When I woke up on Friday, I checked my email before anything else and noticed an email from Tracy at Sunshine Healthcare.

"The Board really wants to keep you guys, and they want to sign before the quarter ends, but our CEO is out next week, so it has to be today. I need four items addressed though, or I can't move forward." Tracy laid out his four sticking points.

The points seemed possible, but these details were not minor. Getting this completed today would involve a major undertaking.

I texted the team and asked everyone to be at the office at 7:00 am. Susie replied privately, "Just a reminder, I have the day off."

Susie had let me know earlier in the week that she needed the day off to take her mother to the doctor. In my way of thinking, this was a very important deal. *Susie has a brother and a sister. Surely one of them could take their mother to the doctor given the circumstances. Come on Susie, I need you.*

We *had* to close this deal! And Susie was my strongest analyst. I replied, "This is urgent. I need you at the office."

Several minutes later, Susie replied, "I'm sorry. I won't be there, but I will work remotely all day except when we're in with the doctor." I felt my face turning red. That would help, but there was no way Susie could do the analysis I needed while working off her laptop without her office setup. I didn't reply, but I began to think of who I could pull from Walter's team to help.

When I texted Walter and asked to borrow an analyst for the day, he offered to let Jan work on our team for the day. She was his strongest analyst, and perhaps the best one in the company. On the one hand, this was great, but on the other it irritated me. This was nothing more than Walter continuing to posture himself as the savior of the deal. Earlier in the week Walter wouldn't help at all, but now – since the renewal looks promising – he's eager to help when he knows that he will benefit personally.

To top it off, he would be viewed as a team player and collaborator, something we both know isn't true. And I, however, won't get the credit I deserve for saving this customer. I tried to put my thoughts aside. I had to focus and push through.

The rest of the team all arrived early and pushed hard through the day. Though Susie wasn't as efficient as if she'd been in the office, she helped Jan get up to speed and also helped to do the analysis. By 4:00 I had the updated proposal in my hands, and, after a hurried review, I sent it off to Tracy and waited.

The tension in the office was tangible, and it seemed like everything in the office moved in slow motion. It would be awful to lose this deal. Retaining this long-term customer, though, would be a big boon for the company. Although we didn't quite get the statement of work where Tracy wanted it, I felt we had made solid concessions and had a great chance at winning this extended contract.

I had my door closed, impatiently monitoring my email and refreshing the send/receive button. As 5:00 approached, I began feeling a knot in my stomach and worrying we may not have won the deal. Susie texted to ask if I had any news. I didn't reply. Through the blinds on my office window, I could see the team begin to pack up their things. Their slow movements and hushed tones said it all. They also worried that we had not done enough, and I found myself blaming Susie. *If Susie was here, we might have been able to hone the numbers better. Jan was great, but Susie just knows the deal better.*

Just as the time on my computer changed to 5:00, an email came in from Tracy.

"Dear Chuck, This looks like a good deal for both of us. The signed proposal is attached."

I jumped up from my seat and burst through my office door! "Sunshine is signed! Tonight, we celebrate! Sandy, call JJ's Bar & Grill and tell them to expect us at 6:30."

The whole office erupted in cheers and applause! After high fives and hugs, almost everyone left the office to hurriedly get home and freshen up for the celebration.

I texted Beth, "Work celebration tonight. I'll be late."

Beth texted back a kissing emoji and the words, "Congratulations!"

I hurriedly began to tie up loose ends on the contract for Sunshine. I was interrupted when Walter walked by my office, leaned against the door frame, and said, "I'm glad I was able to help save that deal." He then pointed his finger at me and did his irritating double click with his tongue as he said, "I'll see you at JJ's."

I could not believe my ears! Walter invited himself to the celebration meant for *my* team. Without doing much more than offering a few suggestions and sharing his analyst for the day, he clearly intended to take full credit for the deal!

I tried to shake it off while I focused on getting this contract to the admin team right away. By the time I made all the changes and reviewed it for accuracy, it was nearly 6:30. I quickly sent it to the admin team and headed out the door to JJ's.

THE WORST CELEBRATION

Even though the restaurant décor hadn't been updated in years, the packed parking lot said it all. Every parking space was filled, and a few cars even parked in the grass. Though tonight was busier than normal, you still couldn't find a slow night at JJ's. JJ's was famous for their good food and easy prices, while the layout appealed to both families and bar customers.

I maneuvered around the horde of hungry people waiting to be seated and looked with hope to the right where I spotted familiar faces. Sandy had reserved the small side room, perfect for our team. They had already set out the appetizers, and most everyone was relaxing and enjoying the celebration, including Walter, who made sure everyone saw him.

I captured everyone's attention with a rhythmic tap on the edge of my glass. "The work on the Sunshine contract has consumed our team's time lately, and rightfully so. It's a crucial deal for us, and we were fighting an uphill battle to retain them. It's because of you – your relentless dedication and hard work saved the deal. And for this, we celebrate! Cheers!"

In chorus, everyone raised their glass and said, "Cheers!"

Over the raised glasses, I noticed Susie walking in. *What is she doing here?* I hadn't even let her know about this, and she hadn't earned the right to celebrate with us, in my mind. As soon as I left the front of the room, I made a beeline to Susie.

"What are you doing here?" I asked. "I thought you needed the day off."

Startled, Susie replied, "That was to take my mom to the doctor. I worked almost—"

Abruptly, I interrupted, "This party is for people who gave their all to winning this deal." I am sure my face showed my emotions, and I turned to walk off.

Walter caught up to me as I reached the other side of the room. He patted me on the back, and said, "Poor gal. Maybe she'll learn we need winners."

As I turned around, I saw Susie grabbing her things and walking out dejected. She may have even wiped a tear from her eye.

I immediately began wrestling with my emotions. *What have I just done?* I did need high performers, but now I realized I had not shown godly love to her at all. I ran through the restaurant and outside to catch her, but she was already gone.

I struggled with my guilt throughout the rest of the celebration and ended up leaving before anyone else, telling them I wasn't feeling my best, which was true, but not for the reasons they imagined.

As soon as I sat down in my car, I texted Susie. "I made a big mistake tonight. I am sorry. Can I buy you coffee in the morning?" She did not reply.

As soon as I walked into the house, Beth asked about the day. Now filled with remorse, I replied, "We won the Sunshine deal. I'll tell you more in a minute. I need to check my email."

I walked straight to my study and checked my messages again for a reply from Susie. Seeing it had been read but not replied to made me feel even more sick. I answered a couple of emails and countersigned the Sunshine contract. Just as I prepared to shut down my laptop, I received a meeting invitation from Susie. Almost simultaneously, she replied to my text, "No. I'll see you at 8:00 on Monday. I've sent an invite."

I moped into the living room and asked Beth if we could talk.

"Sure, are you okay?" Beth asked.

"Honey, I made a big mistake today. Do you remember Susie? The analyst at work?"

"Yeah, the short brunette? Maybe forty?"

"Yeah, that's her. I think I really hurt her today." I then told Beth all about the day, starting with the text this morning and Susie's reply. I continued through the pressures of getting the details of the deal together, and the victory of the signed contract with Sunshine and the celebration party.

Beth said, "It seems like Susie did what she could."

"Yeah. She did." I replied. "But I didn't see it that way. I saw it as a lack of loyalty. That was my first big mistake. It gets worse though. She showed up at the celebration, and I told her the celebration was for people who gave their all."

Astounded, Beth said, "Chuck! Why would you do that?"

Defensively, I replied, "I know how it looks, but I thought it was right in that moment. As soon as I saw her leave, I knew I'd messed up. I've apologized already, and Susie and I are going to talk on Monday."

Dumbfounded, Beth sat there quietly. She finally said, "You can be a bit … intense sometimes."

I didn't say anything as I got up and went back to my study.

I texted Barry, "Can we meet for coffee tomorrow?"

Barry replied, "Let's meet at my office instead. 7:00? Text when you arrive, and I'll let you in the side door."

I wondered why Barry wanted to meet at his office, especially on a Saturday, but I answered, "Sure. See you then."

A DIFFERENT WAY

I had never been to Barry's office, though I knew its location, in a three-story, nondescript building. I thought maybe his company had offices on the top floor.

After parking near Barry's truck, I texted him and made my way to the side door. Barry opened it just before I arrived.

"Welcome, Chuck! There are a few people working today. We're trying to wrap up a project, but I thought it might be more private here."

Barry walked me through the lobby to the elevator. As he pressed 3, I asked, "How many other companies office here?"

"It's only us. Training rooms and the kitchen are on the ground floor. Administration, sales, and our trainers are on the second floor. And the rest of us are on the third floor."

I did not realize his company employed so many.

As we walked out of the elevator, we took a right and walked to the end of the hall. The neat and tidy offices had glass walls like mine at Southside. Barry had the corner office with a small four-top conference table, a couch and two chairs. He had a large leather chair behind a large desk with two more chairs facing the desk.

Pointing at one of chairs across from the couch, Barry said, "Have a seat, Chuck. I'm going to grab us some coffee."

After Barry walked out, I noticed nearly indiscernible music playing softly in the background. I then noticed the painting above the couch. In the center, a small, forked stream flowed from top to bottom, flanked by large rocks that were begging to be sat upon. To the stream's left, a dirt path meandered, while tall grasses, dotted with a profusion of wildflowers, filled the spaces beyond the path and to the stream's right. It was serene.

Just then Barry walked back in. He handed me a coffee mug as he said, "This isn't quite as good as The Uncommon Brew, but I think it will do. Sorry, it's only half full. I just started a fresh pot."

As he sat down, he said, "Tell me what's on your mind."

I began to recount the week at a high level until I reached Friday's climax. I then told him the details about what happened with Susie, and finished up by saying, "I really messed up, Barry. I feel like this was a test, and I failed."

Barry sat there quietly for a moment as he drank a bit of his coffee and stared out a window over my shoulder. He set his coffee mug down then looked me in the eyes and asked, "Do you want me to tell you what you need to hear or what you want to hear?"

"What I need to hear." I replied.

"I don't mentor someone until I think they are ready. But like Jesus said, 'The spirit is willing, but the flesh is weak.' I can tell your spirit is ready to mature, but your flesh is weak. I think you're on the right track though. But, from what you've told me, you work in a toxic environment. Unfortunately, when good people stay in a toxic environment, the toxic environment often wins."

Defensively, I replied, "But no place is perfect."

"You're right, but toxic isn't normal, even by the world's standards. You may be the one to make a change there, but if that's so, it's going to take prayer, a place for you to recharge and learn, and Christian friends with whom you can be honest and are committed to keep you in check. Even then, it's dangerous."

Barry continued, "Think on that a moment. The coffee should be done now. I'm going to go refill our cups."

While Barry was gone, I prayed for God's help. I couldn't leave Southside. There was nowhere else I could make this kind of money.

Barry walked back in and handed me a fresh cup of coffee. He then shared more about the importance of prayer and being surrounded by believers, even in the best of environments.

We both had a sip of our coffee, then I replied, "I guess that's why I like our coffee talks so much."

"They're nice," Barry said, "but I'm not sure they're enough."

He took another drink of his coffee, then set the mug down on the table between our chairs. "We began this study on the Fruit of the Spirit because you saw something different, and you wanted it. Love is the first virtue of the Fruit of the Spirit, but remember how I told you I also think it's the master virtue. Without love, none of the rest matters. Ultimately, the Fruit of the Spirit is an outside example of an inside change. The reality is that if your life doesn't exemplify the Fruit of the Spirit, you're still an immature Christian."

I let that soak in a minute, then I replied, "I think I get it. I know I'm still immature, but I'm also growing."

"Let's close in prayer." We bowed our heads as Barry said, "Father, You know this man's heart and his desire for more of You. Grant him wisdom as he grows in You and protect him from the attacks of the enemy. I especially pray for this situation with Susie, that You'll help him repair this damage and You will be glorified through this. Amen."

We both finished our coffees, then Barry walked me out. As I left Kene Business Advisors, I thought a lot about what Barry had said. As I sat down in my car, I realized how much we had covered. I opened up my journal and made a lot of notes. I concluded with, "Am I showing God's love at Southside, or is Southside destroying me?" Tears welled up in my eyes as I sat there. I realized Southside had been destroying me, but I also felt I could be a positive influence there. *Was I strong enough to be the positive influence? Yes, but only with God. My lapses were because I was trying to do this on my own.*

When I arrived home, Beth asked, "How was it?"

"Barry really gave me a lot to think about. I feel better, but I'm going to spend time this weekend praying about the situation with Susie. Oh, and I want to go to church tomorrow."

Beth smiled. "Me too."

Church was good. It always was. Pastor Ken preached on prayer, which seemed uncanny. As we left, Barry and Dona caught us. Barry put his hand on my shoulder and said, "I'm praying for you, brother."

"Thank you, Barry. I need it."

He replied, "We all do."

CROSSED THE LINE

The next morning, I arrived at the office early. And so did Susie. I didn't say anything to her, thinking it was best to wait for the meeting. At 8:00 she knocked on my door. I stood up and said, "Please, Susie, come in."

After she sat down, I started, "Susie. I am sorry. The way I acted Friday was embarrassing. I am trying to be a better person, but I blew it."

Susie looked at me, tears in her eyes. "Yes, you did. Friday was a very important day. I was taking mom to the doctor to hear the results of her bloodwork. She's been very sick lately. We've been worried it might be cancer."

"I'm sorry, Susie, I had no idea."

"Well, the good news is she's going to be fine." Susie paused and pulled a letter out of her notebook. She handed it to me and said, "But the bad news is I'm turning in my notice. I realized on Friday that I don't really matter to you or to Southside. I've been a dedicated employee for a long time, and I've put up with a lot. I was really struggling with how you treated me Friday morning, but the way you talked to me at the celebration crossed a line."

I quickly replied, "Susie—"

She interrupted me, "It's too late, Chuck. You've told me you're sorry. Even if you don't mean it, I still forgive you, but I can't stay here. I'll finish out my two weeks, and I'll be sure whoever takes on my role has all they need to succeed."

She then got up and walked out of my office, shutting my door quietly behind her.

I didn't know how to respond. This should be a good day at the office after closing the Sunshine deal, but I just wanted to be left alone. I kept my door shut all day so I wouldn't have to talk to anyone.

I had brought my journal to work, something I had never done before. I had intended to read through my notes, not knowing how much I would need that today. Toward the end of the day I finally pulled it out and the last words I had written stood out. Right now I felt like a failure, but through God, I could be a better influence here.

I did something I had not done before. I journaled about what had happened today and how I could have better shown love. I then wrote down something I remembered Barry saying, "Be a good reflection of Jesus." This almost felt like prayer. I closed my notebook and headed home.

The next morning, I was anxious to talk to Barry. I was hoping he had some advice that would help.

As I drove to the coffee shop, I noticed the first trees were starting to change colors. It reminded me of the changes in my life. Soon these leaves would fall, but after another season, new growth would begin again.

We arrived at the coffee shop at the same time, and I paid for our coffee, dropping $5 in the tip jar. Barry and I then sat down, and he asked, "How are you, and how did the meeting with Susie go?"

I told Barry about Susie quitting. After listening to me, he said, "I expected this might happen after what you told me Saturday. You were hard on her. You're not going to repair this damage overnight, but you have an opportunity to show her God's love over the next two weeks."

"How do I do that?" I asked.

"First, I don't think I'd ask her to stay again. That will undermine and maybe even influence how you react. Second, I'd treat her just like you treat everyone else – I hope that will be better than what you've told me about.

Third, I'd throw a going-away party. You said she's been with Southside a while."

"Yeah, a lot longer than me," I replied.

"She deserves it then. Finally, if it were me, I'd give her a handwritten note as she leaves on her last day, thanking her for her service with Southside, recounting your appreciation for her, and once again apologizing."

I pulled out my journal – the last words I had written were, "Be a good reflection of Jesus." How uncanny. Right after that, I added, " – TODAY." I made a few more notes about what Barry said. I didn't want to forget this. The next two weeks would be a great opportunity to show God's love.

Barry took a sip of his coffee as he waited on me. Once I finished, he continued, "It's been almost three months since we started talking, and we've covered a lot. Love is a topic you could study endlessly. Like I said Saturday, I think it's the master virtue. But now we're at the end of our dedicated study on Love. I want to end with a couple more things. And next week, I'd like to meet one more time on this so you can tell me what you've learned."

Caught off guard, I asked, "Aren't we going to have coffee again after next week?"

"Of course we are. We'll talk about that next week though." Barry took a sip of his coffee, then continued, "One of the first verses I gave you to look up was Galatians 5:14."

I asked, "Is that where it says to love your neighbor as yourself?"

"You've got it," Barry said. "You'll find those same words elsewhere in the Bible. I encourage you to look it up. In one of those passages – Matthew 22:39 – it's called the second greatest commandment."

He then winked at me as he said, "That means there's another more important. You should look that up too."

I wrote that down.

As if he was finishing a story, Barry concluded, "Finally, we have Romans 13:8, where we're told to owe no one anything except love."

I made a note of this verse in my notebook as Barry paused. When I looked up, he had taken the last drink of his coffee. I finished mine too, then, knowing our time today was over, I took our cups to the tray in the corner.

We walked out together. As Barry neared his truck, he looked at me and said, "I continue to have you in my prayers, Chuck. And I mean that."

REAL CHANGE

On the way to work I realized something had changed. I couldn't quite put my finger on it, but I knew the world was going to see the new Chuck from this day forward.

When I arrived at the office, I noticed Susie had taken down some of her cube decorations. The reminder was gut wrenching.

I sat down at my computer and immediately emailed Sandy, asking her to make sure we prepared treats and a cookie cake for Susie's last day. I then ordered some professional stationery to write Susie a letter.

The rest of the week continued to be no less stressful than prior days had been, especially since we were still trying to close another new deal, but I never lost my temper, even when others made mistakes. When the team closed a mid-sized deal by adding new services to an existing contract, I took them all out to lunch and recognized each of their contributions.

Thursday night when I walked into the house, I gave Beth a single rose followed by a hug and a kiss, "I appreciate you, Beth."

Surprised, Beth asked, "Is everything okay?"

"Yes, it is. I just wanted you to know how much you mean to me," I replied.

I needed to work, but I took time to eat with Beth and the kids before heading to my study. This "new me" felt good.

Although the fall colors were just starting to appear, I told Beth and the kids at supper that I wanted to take them on a drive through the country on Saturday. The boys groaned, but Abby and Beth seemed happy about it.

On Saturday morning, we packed a picnic lunch and took the Escalade for an early autumn tour. We stopped at a little beach on the lake for lunch, and the boys learned to skip rocks as Abby picked Asters and made a bouquet for Beth. We even had a peaceful drive back home.

PASSING THE TORCH

At church on Sunday, Pastor Ken preached about serving one another in love – another timely message. I truly enjoyed it.

Afterward, Dona walked up to us on the way out, "Barry and I are going out to lunch with a few other families. If you'd like to join us, we're eating at the Mexican restaurant just up the street."

Beth answered, "We'd love to, Dona, but we've got the kids."

Dona laughed, "Come on, Beth, you feed them, don't you?"

Beth chuckled a bit, and then looked at me. I replied, "Maybe next time."

Dona replied, "Okay, suit yourself!"

All afternoon I wished we had accepted the invitation. We weren't used to things like this though, so I made a mental note to be ready next time. I did put the time to good use, however, and began to think through all I had learned about love.

After making a lot of notes, I finally put together my thoughts in one succinct paragraph, which I wrote in my journal.

I felt eager to meet with Barry on Tuesday and arrived early to chat with Annie until I saw Barry pull in. I then paid for our coffees, dropped a $20 in the tip jar, and sat down. Barry walked in and sat down just as Annie brought out our coffees.

She looked at me and said, "Thank you, Chuck. You didn't have to do that."

I winked at her as I replied, "Bless you, Annie."

As Annie walked off, Barry said, "You seem to be in a better place. Was your week better?"

"It sure was. I feel as if something has shifted – as if I don't have to try so hard to demonstrate love, and I like it!"

Barry took a sip of his coffee and said, "Mmm, that's delicious!" He gave Annie a thumbs up, then he continued, "That's really good to hear, my friend. Just be careful though. Growing in the Spirit doesn't often come without setbacks, and they can be discouraging. You're still going to mess up, maybe bad. When it happens, don't get down about it. Don't be afraid to call either. When you're going through tough times, it helps to talk it out."

"I'll remember that Barry, but I think this episode with Susie has really changed me."

"Good," he replied.

Barry took another sip of his coffee, then he said, "You had an assignment this week. I want to hear what you've learned about love."

I opened up my journal and read to Barry what I wrote:

"God is love, and without love we cannot know Him. The two greatest commandments are to love God with everything we have and to love our neighbors as ourselves. This is an active love, not a passive love, and it is modeled in 1 Corinthians 13. This kind of love doesn't commit evil against a neighbor. And a love like this is the fulfillment of the Law."

"You've got it, Chuck!" Barry replied.

Encouraged by his enthusiasm, I continued. "That's not all! I ran across one other thing I want to share with you. Check this out!"

"1 John 4:8 says God is love. John 10:30 says Jesus and God are one. Matthew 5:17 says Jesus came to fulfill the law and the prophets. Finally, Romans 13:10 says that love is the fulfillment of the Law. So, get this: God equals love, and Jesus equals God. So, Jesus is love. Love fulfills the Law, and Jesus fulfills the Law. It all makes sense!"

"That's a great find! I don't think I've ever noticed that before!" Barry replied. He asked me to repeat it all so he could write it down.

"I really feel like I've learned a lot, but I also feel like I have a lot more to learn."

Barry replied, "We always have a lot more to learn! You've come a long way though. I mentioned last week that this is the end of our dedicated study on love, although it is just the beginning of your study on the Fruit of the Spirit."

He continued, "Let's talk a bit about what's going to happen next. If you're ready to continue your studies, I'd like to continue to mentor you, but I want to introduce you to another member of Noble Bereans. His name is Mark, and he's going to teach you about the next attribute of the Fruit of the Spirit."

"Joy?" I asked.

"That's right. Are you ready?" Barry asked.

I replied, "To be honest, Barry, I'd rather learn from you. But I trust you. I'm ready."

"Great. Let's have lunch at my house Sunday, and I'll introduce you to Mark, and then we'll meet back here next week."

Barry stood up and took our coffee cups to the counter. Even though I knew we'd meet here again next week, it felt different this time. As Barry walked back toward me, I stuck out my hand. When he took hold of it, I leaned in for a hug. "Thank you, Barry. I look forward to the next step."

MEET THE AUTHOR

My parents raised me in a home where we made church a regular part of our lives and I embraced Jesus at the age of 12. Yet, it took the journey into adulthood for my faith to truly unfold and to sharpen my sense of purpose within my faith.

I always knew I had been called to serve God, but I grappled with the meaning of serving God. Through seeking God and prayer, the answer crystallized for me: *I serve God by urging fellow believers to reflect the light of Jesus into their corners of the world.* We are not meant to be hidden! We are to live boldly with our lives marked by the vibrant fruits of transformation.

A significant turning point for me happened when I took time for a mission trip with my home-based church to teach Choctaw children about the Fruit of the Spirit. I realized that God had given us this model of what the Christian life should look like.

While I value traditional church, I've found a powerful connection in the close-knit fabric of home-based churches. They offer fertile ground for nurturing a relational and tangible faith, one that blooms in the everyday alongside others.

I possess an unwavering dedication to scripture and strive to be a serious student of the Bible, delving into the original languages and historical contexts to better understand God's grand mosaic.

Inspired by the Noble Bereans in Acts 17:11, I've embarked on a mission to encourage others to seek the same earnest and noble examination of the Scriptures. I firmly believe we must all be equipped both to question and to understand the foundations of our faith.

In the end, I hope to weave these threads – my understanding of faith, my insights from Scripture, and the simplicity of Christ's teachings – into stories that not only entertain but also inspire growth and reflection.

I am a tried-and-true "Gen Xer." I grew up staying out late, riding bikes and catching lightning bugs. I saw the dawn of MTV and still remain convinced that the best music is the Eighties music.

I grew up thinking I might be a chef one day, but the twists and turns of life often take us to places we never imagined. After a stint in the restaurant business, I tried my hand at sales, factory work, and a long list of other jobs before finding a passion for cybersecurity. Now I serve as the Chief Risk & Information Security Officer for a major fintech provider.

I'm happily married to my childhood sweetheart who stole my heart at just 15-years-old. It didn't take us long to realize we wanted to spend the rest of our lives together. God has blessed us with three terrific sons, a lovely daughter-in-law, and a grandson who is a highlight of our lives with another grandchild on the way.

Want to connect with Steve Sanders and explore more about his work?

Scan the QR code below to access exclusive content, updates, and insights!